THE GUARDIAN'S LEGACY

THE GUARDIAN'S LEGACY

Coin of Time Series | Book 1

LUCIANA CAVALLARO

Mythos | Publications

Mythos Publications
www.luccav.com

Publisher's Note: This is a work of fiction. Names, characters, places, and incidents are a product of the author's imagination. Locales and public names are sometimes used for atmospheric purposes. Any re-semblance to actual people, living or dead, or to businesses, companies, events, institutions, or locales is completely coincidental.

Cover artwork: Damonza.com

The Guardian's Legacy/ Luciana Cavallaro. — 1st ed.

ISBN 978-0-6452726-1-1

Prologue

A gun fired and a bullet whizzed by as he swerved, his feet pounding the grass. His breathing sounded harsh and loud in his ears as he willed himself to run faster. Alongside, his companion kept up with him. He glanced at her. She didn't look frightened, except her face was tense, her cheeks flushed and her breathing shallow and noisy.

Another shot rang out.

'*Mon dieu!*'

'Are you hit?' he asked, his voice higher than usual.

'*Non!*' She checked over her shoulder. 'We need to get out of this clearing and into that line of trees.'

They zigzagged across the expansive green lawn, one a grounds-keeper at a golf club would envy, and headed for the cluster of pine trees edging the boundary of the castle. More shots rang out and a dull droning of engines came from behind them.

The woman swore. 'Motorbikes.'

He glanced back and saw three helmeted riders emerge from the long driveway of the Gothic-style castle, exhaust fumes pluming like tufts of dirty clouds as the motorbikes raced towards them.

They sprinted to the trees. Behind them, the throttle of the motorbikes roared as they gained ground. Bullets tore into the tree trunks around them, spitting bark into the air. They ran into the shelter of the forest, pushing through the undergrowth, heedless of the low branches that whipped their arms and legs.

Then they were falling headlong down a ravine. The man tumbled as if he were a load of clothes in a washing machine, crushing twigs and leaves as his weight and gravity propelled him downwards. He fell into a shallow ditch at the base of the hill. Battered and streaked in fine lines of cuts, he lay winded, unable to move. Then he gasped as his companion landed on top of him.

'Nik, are you all right?'

He opened his eyes and looked up into the anxious face of the woman sprawled on top of him. 'I think so. Your head has a gash, Alexandrie.' Nik wiped the blood from her forehead. 'Thank goodness, it's not deep.'

They gazed at each other, the enormity of their near-death experience overwhelming. Nik gave her a lopsided grin and was about to say how fortunate they were when Alexandrie's mouth descended on his. The fervour of her kiss surprised him. Nik responded to her passionate and hungry kiss, wrapping his arms around her.

Alexandrie broke the kiss, her pupils dilating. Nik reached to capture her mouth. This was nothing like they had shared before. It was as if his body had woken from a deep slumber and every pore tingled with anticipation.

She covered his mouth with a hand. 'Listen!' she said, in an urgent whisper.

Nik's ears strained and then he heard.

'They never give up!'

'We need to get out of here.'

Alexandrie scrambled off him and bolted upright. Nik winced as he struggled to get up, his body aching from head to toe, his limbs refusing to obey his brain. She grabbed his hand and pulled him up.

'Use the coin!' she urged.

'Are you sure?'

'Yes! They're getting closer!'

'Don't let go of my hand,' Nik warned.

The rumble of the motorbikes was almost on them. There were shouts in Slovak as their assailants drew closer.

'Quick, Nik!'

He glanced up at the levee from where they had fallen, the riders coming into view. One of the pursuers pointed down at them and started down the slope. Nik tossed the grey, irregularly shaped coin into the air. They watched as it flipped upwards and a gust of wind buffeted it. The coin shifted and spiralled downwards. Nik caught the treasured coin and closed it tight in his fist.

A sea of blackness swallowed him. A rush of wind blasted his body and threatened to wrench his limbs from their sockets. His lungs burned as they struggled to draw air. The wind plucked him into the air, and like the jet stream of a plane, catapulted him into the void. He was engulfed in a soundless space, and accelerating at breakneck speeds.

Oomph! Nik fell flat on his face, his arms and legs spread like a five-pointed star. Dazed, he lay there, not moving. He could feel the warm sun on his arms and head. He tried to open his eyes, but they felt as if glue sealed them shut, and when he attempted to move his arms and legs, they resisted much like an immovable boulder. If he could shout he would, but only managed a grunt instead.

'It's not every day one sees a man fall from the sky!' said a gruff voice.

Powerful hands grabbed Nik and turned him onto his back.

'Hello? Can you hear me?' Nik's eyelids fluttered as a hand, its palm coarse, slapped his cheek. 'Let me check and see if you broke any bones. That was quite a drop. Did you insult the gods, by chance?'

Nik prised his dry lips apart. 'Ug …' He clenched a hand, and with it beach sand. He smelt the briny air of the sea and frowned, his mind muddied. Where am I?

'Hmm … I'll be right back,' the man said. Nik heard him leave, the sand crunching with each step. Nik lay there, recalling the alarm raised by Resnick's men and being chased into the forest.

Minutes passed when he heard the man return and lift his head, placing a clay vessel to his mouth. Nik spluttered and coughed as water caught in his throat. He leaned on his side, still choking, and collapsed back onto the ground. He opened his eyes and stared at the cloudless blue sky.

'Who are you?' the man asked, his face looming over Nik.

Nik sat up panicked, whipping his head from side to side. 'Where is Alexandrie?' he asked. His gaze fell on the bearded man who wore a dress. A dress? No, it's a khiton. Nik struggled to his knees and glanced around at the sparse coastline. No tall buildings or vehicles anywhere. Behind the older man, a donkey brayed. Startled, Nik slumped onto his backside.

The man steadied Nik and frowned. 'There is no-one else here, just you and I.'

'Who the heck are you?'

'Why, I am Herodotos.'

Chapter One

Nikolaos Zosimos opened the door to the office he shared with the other teachers. He sighed with relief when the door closed behind him and the noise of the students and their lockers opening and clanging shut for the next round of classes was reduced to a dull hum. He placed his laptop, books and work collected from his Year 7 History class on his desk and sat down. The stack of papers beckoned and taunted him to start marking them. Ignoring the assessments, he opened a drawer and checked his mobile for messages. His mother had sent a reminder for dinner on Friday night, and there was a message from his grandfather Iasos.

Nik put the phone back in the drawer. His grandfather's text message struck him as odd, but he didn't give it another thought, and turned his attention to his timetable. He had a period of DOTT, duties other than teaching, before his next class. For the next twenty minutes, he rifled through a batch of answers to a pop quiz and did a quick scan of the answers.

'How depressing,' he said as he dropped the last sheet of paper on the pile.

'What's wrong?' Rachel glanced over at him.

'I need to revise the section on primary and secondary sources, and how historians and archaeologists use them for investigating history.'

'My class had the same issue.'

'Okay, so we need to simplify and create a practical lesson. Tomorrow, I'll take my class out for a walk along the river and point out the differences between the two,' Nik said. 'I'll work on that later. My Year 12 Ancient History class is next, and we're studying the destruction of Troy.' He grinned. 'I've got them reading Homer's *Iliad*. You should have heard them complaining after reading the first few lines.'

Rachel laughed. 'The English Department will love you for that.'

He nodded. 'I've teed up with Christina to come to my class to teach them the technical elements of the story.'

'Nice. Your class will whine even more!' she said with a guffaw.

'They'll thank me when they sit their last exam.'

His mobile phone beeped again. Nik opened his drawer and picked it up. He frowned.

Niko, can you come to my house tonight? There is something I need to discuss with you. Papou

Nik's heart missed a beat. He messaged back, his nimble fingers flying.

Hi Papou, I'll be there as soon as I can get away from work. Is everything ok? Niko

He put the phone on the desk and stared at it, willing it to ping with a new message. His mind was going over the worst possible scenarios. He wished his grandfather would hurry and message back. He and his grandfather shared a love for ancient history and it had been he who encouraged Nik to study the classics at school and then at university. They'd spend many hours in the week chatting about what Nik was learning and the relationship of the past to what was happening in the world.

The school bell rang. He gathered his textbooks and laptop, put the phone in his pocket, and headed for the door. About to turn the doorknob, he hesitated and returned to his desk. He locked the phone in the drawer. If it was something serious, his grandfather would have replied. Besides, students weren't allowed to bring their phones into class; he wouldn't be a suitable role model if he turned up to class with his.

For Nik, the next two lessons before lunchtime seemed to drag. On his return to the office, he checked his mobile for messages. Nothing. After lunch, in his last two classes of the day, the students' subdued responses to his questions reinforced his anxious mood. As soon as the bell rang, Nik dismissed his class. He gathered his things and locked the door to the classroom on his way out. He dodged students, open lockers and bags as he made his way to the office. Other members of his department hadn't arrived yet. He slipped the laptop into its carry bag and shoved the pile of assessment papers collected from his classes into his briefcase. The door opened and a few other staff members filed in, chatting after their last lessons for the day. The person he wanted to speak with was the last to arrive. He walked over as the Head of the Humanities Department placed his books on his desk.

'May I speak with you, Leonard?'

The short, older man gazed up at him. 'What is it, Nik?'

'I got a strange text from my granddad earlier, and he hasn't replied to the one I sent. Would you mind if I leave? I know we have our department meeting and it may well be nothing, but I'm concerned something has happened.'

'I understand. Go check on your grandfather.'

'Thanks.'

Nik collected his bags, said goodbye to his colleagues and rushed out the door. With his keys in one hand and phone in the other, he threaded his way through a crowd of boisterous and energetic adolescent boys at their lockers. Oblivious of their raucous banter, Nik scrolled through the contact list on his phone and hit the call function. The line was engaged. With a quick flick of his thumb, he chose another number. This time the line rang.

'Afternoon, sir.'

'Night, sir.'

Nik acknowledged the boys with a nod. 'See you tomorrow, boys.'

'Hello?'

'Hi Mum.'

'Nik, how are you? You haven't called to cancel dinner tomorrow night?'

'No, I'm still coming.'

A few more students called out to Nik, to which he responded.

'Are you at school?' his mother asked.

'I'm just leaving. Did Papou call you today?'

'No, why?'

'He tried calling earlier and then left a message asking me to see him tonight. I thought he may have called you.'

'I haven't spoken to him for a few days. What about your father? Did you ring him?'

'I did, but his phone was busy. Though I can't see Papou ringing Dad for anything.'

Nik unlocked his car, placed his laptop and briefcase on the back seat, and got in behind the steering wheel.

'Your father attempts to keep in touch with your grandfather, but you know their relationship isn't good. Did he say why he wanted you to visit?'

'I'll find out soon enough, I'm heading over there now,' Nik said. He paused and then added, 'It's odd for Papou to ring during the day when I'm at work. He wouldn't call unless he's unwell, would he?'

'Iasos is one of the healthiest men of his age I know,' his mother said, 'and in all the years I have known him he has seldom been sick. I reckon it's something different he wants to discuss.'

'Any ideas on what?'

She laughed. 'With Iasos and his varied interests, who knows?'

They spoke for a few minutes more before Nik said goodbye and drove out of the staff car park and off the school grounds.

Chapter Two

'Hello? Papou? Are you home?' Nik called as he knocked on the fly-screen door.

He took in the red-painted porch, white railing and two rattan chairs concealed from the street behind a canopy of roses, the yellow blooms and a few buds still on show though beginning to wane in the final summer month. The chairs brought memories of his grandmother sitting there in the afternoons, neighbours stopping by to chat and have a cup of coffee. He could feel her presence whenever he popped over after work, something he had done often as a teenager and into his adulthood. He missed her. She always fussed over him, filling him up with home-cooked food.

A shadowy figure appeared at the end of the darkened passage. 'Hi, Papou.' Nik smiled.

'Niko!' The old man moved with slow and steady steps, his grizzled face lit up as he neared the doorway. 'It's good to see you, my boy. Glad you could come.'

Nik heard the familiar click as Papou unlocked the screen door. He took a step to the side as his grandfather pushed the door open.

'Your text message sounded urgent. I was worried something was wrong.'

His grandfather grinned, the years falling away as the sparkle of joy gleamed in his light blue eyes. 'Come on in,' he said with a quick, jerky wave of his hand.

Nik stepped over the threshold and gave him a hug. His grandfather, on the cusp of turning eighty, still looked robust He had a full head of hair, grey with flecks of brown; a tall handsome man in good health. In his youth, he'd had many women pursuing him. Nik was grateful for being part of the gene pool. He was nearing thirty, with a head full of inky hair and blue eyes, and could pass for twenty. So said his female cousins of the same age, who couldn't understand why he was still single, despite their many attempts to set him up with their girlfriends and acquaintances.

'What did you want to discuss?' he asked, stepping inside.

'All in time, Niko. Let's sit at the back under the trees. It's nice and cool outside,' his grandfather replied as he locked the door.

'I've always loved it out there,' Nik said. He followed Iasos through the hallway, the walls lined with family photographs, in colour and black and white.

'Go get a few beers from the fridge on the back verandah,' his grandfather said. 'I'll be with you in a moment.'

Nik refrained from saying any more. He knew pressuring his grandfather would get him nowhere. He pushed the back fly-screen door open and sauntered over to the old yellow Kelvinator refrigerator. Though rusty at the corners and along the base, the fridge still kept the drinks chilled. He slipped four stubbies into an ancient esky and shut the lid. Nik spied his grandfather with a tray of food and hurried over to the door to pull it open. There was a bowl of green and black olives, eggplant dip with gyros, keftedakia – small meatballs – and crispy whitebait deep-fried and coated in savoury flour. It looked like Iasos had prepared the meze platter, a mixture of hot and cold appetisers, for this visit.

They walked over to the jarrah outdoor setting, under the

canopy of an old willow tree. His grandfather placed the tray on the table as Nik pulled out two beers, unscrewed the lids, handed one over to his grandfather and then sat.

Nik raised his stubby. 'Cheers, Papou.'

'*Stin ygeiá sas*, cheers.' Papou took a mouthful of beer and turned to Nik. 'Eat. You must be hungry after teaching those rowdy boys.'

Nik had to smile. In his day he hadn't always been an exemplary student and had given his teachers a hard time, but mostly, the boys in his own classes were well behaved. Like everyone else, kids had unpleasant days, and combined with hormones, it could create behavioural issues. He picked up a meatball and popped it into his mouth.

He relaxed as they chatted about the weather, politics, the former premier of Western Australia and the revolving door of federal leaders of the Australian parliament. They moved on to history, a favourite subject of theirs, in particular the ancient world. His grandfather was an intellectual who spoke six languages and had been a professor of ancient history at the university in Perth. He had retired a few years ago to write a book on the history of their family. When Nik asked about the progress of the book, his grandfather remained secretive, saying that when the time was right, he would show him.

Nik tore off a piece of flatbread to scoop up the eggplant dip. The roasted vegetable blended with crushed garlic and oil complemented the toasted gyros.

'I'm glad you came,' Papou said, gazing at Nik.

'So what is it you want to talk over?' Nik noted the serious expression on his grandfather's face and his heart plummeted. 'You're not dying, are you? I was concerned and rang Mum to find out whether she'd heard from you ...'

Papou smiled and patted Nik's hand, cutting him off.

'No, Niko, I'm not dying. However, I have something for you. It's been in the family for a long time, a very long time.'

'Thank goodness! Ever since your text I thought you were sick, ill, and you wanted to share the news with me. I'm very relieved you're okay.' His heartbeat returned to normal. 'What is it you want to give me?'

'I didn't mean to worry you, but it was important that you came.' Papou reached into his pocket and pulled out a coin. 'I want you to take care of this.'

Nik peered at the dulled silver coin. The shape was irregular, not a proper circle but the shape obvious. The face of the coin had a turtle, the workmanship refined with the shell outlined in intricate detail, as were the head and flippers.

'What's on the other side?' he asked, reaching out to turn over the coin.

His grandfather closed his hand, the unusual coin closeted in his fist. Nik looked at him with an arched brow.

'First, I must tell you the history of the coin, and how it came to be in our family's possession.'

Nik gazed at his grandfather, but the expression on the old man's face gave nothing away. 'Okay,' he said, pointing to the coin with his stubby, 'so how old is the coin?'

Papou held it up between his thumb and index finger. 'It's two and a half thousand years old.'

'No way!' Nik perched on the edge of his seat to inspect it.

Papou nodded. 'According to primary historical accounts, it was minted in 500 BCE, on the island of Aegina. See the imprint of the turtle? It's the symbol of the goddess Aphrodite, and according to a handful of scholars, the Temple of Aphrodite issued the coin. The island had the first mint in the world, and in honour of the goddess they struck the coins with this image.'

'It must be worth a fortune,' said Nik, awed. 'Have you ever had it valued?'

His grandfather shook his head. 'No. It is a part of our family's history. You must never sell it.' Papou took hold of Nik's arm and grasped it. His grip tightened as his eyes hardened like ice. 'This coin has remained in the family for two millennia and will continue to do so. Do I make myself clear?'

'Chill, Papou,' Nik said, shocked by the harshness of the old man's voice and grim tone, let alone the vice-like grip on his arm. 'What's the harm in knowing how much it's worth?'

'Its value is greater than money. Our family are the guardians of the coin.'

'Guardians? Of a two thousand five hundred-year-old coin?'

'The significance of this coin has more layers than an onion,' his grandfather said in a sombre tone. 'Many people have searched for it. Even Hitler had his soldiers seeking the coin.'

Nik felt a cold shiver snake up his spine. 'Why did Hitler want it?'

'It is said that the unique qualities of the coin can change the life of the one who possesses it.'

'How?'

'It goes back to the first person who learned what it can do,' Papou said as he pocketed the coin. He took a long draught of beer. 'Hand me another, will you?'

Nik took another stubby from the esky. 'Who was it?' he asked as he handed over the bottle.

'Herodotos.'

'The ancient Greek historian?'

Papou nodded and smiled with approval. 'I am very pleased you have the same passion for the past as I have and studied ancient history.'

'I wrote a paper at university on Herodotos to disprove why scholars considered him a charlatan who fabricated history.'

'That is why I chose you. The knowledge you have will serve you well. However, you must learn much more if you are to be the guardian of this coin,' said Papou. 'You will be prepared, and understand how important it is to protect the coin. There are aspects of this role you must consider before you agree to become the coin's next protector.' The old man regarded Nik, his gaze unyielding.

When he resumed speaking, there was no inflection in his voice. His tone sounded like the emotionless voice that recites the many options when calling an insurance or telecommunications company. 'The coin's custodian must undertake further studies on the history of Ancient Greece, and I'm not referring to accessing information from the internet. There are books and instructions passed on from the current protector to the next, and there is also training with weapons.'

Nik did a double take. 'Weapons training? What weapons are you referring to, and why do I need to learn how to use them? I can't see how protecting a coin warrants such extreme measures.'

'This is serious, my boy.' Papou's eyes flashed and become flinty. 'There are many people who will do anything to get their hands on this tribute coin. You think Hitler was the only one who learned of its existence? The world would be very different if he had found it. Several guardians have lost their lives protecting the goddess's turtle.'

'If there are, as you say, many people who know of its existence, how is it not mentioned in the history books or anywhere else?'

'Our family worked hard to discount its existence, and the only ones who knew the truth of it were the guardians. They alone know the power it holds and what it can do.' Papou shook his finger at Nik. 'And that is how it will remain. No one except the protector and his or her successor is aware of the coin's existence and purpose.'

'And you've chosen me to be the next person to guard the coin?' Nik ran his thumb over the mouth of the beer bottle. 'I'm guessing Dad hasn't been told?'

His grandfather did not answer straight away, instead his jaw tightened. 'Not every potential guardian is suitable, or dependable, to take the responsibility. It is at the discretion of the current caretaker to determine who should be the coin's next protector.'

Nik's father had spent his youth and early adulthood in a drug-fuelled haze. In several instances he was fortunate not to have died from an overdose. To get him away from the group of people he was mixing with, Papou had sent his son to a family in Greece. The village was small and remote, high in the mountains of Taygetos. It was there that he had met Nik's mother.

'Did Yiayiá learn of the secret?'

Papou's face softened at the mention of his wife. 'She was a very intelligent woman. I know she knew about the coin throughout our marriage. She knew me better than I did myself.'

'Did she ever ask you?'

'No, nor did she speak of it. She was a wise and beautiful woman.'

'I miss her too,' Nik said. His attention turned to the gazebo Papou had built for his grandmother early in their marriage. She would sit in it every day, even if it was only for a few minutes. 'Apart from our shared interest in ancient history, why did you pick me?'

'You are smart, a quick learner and able to think, using logic and being creative where necessary. You will need these attributes to protect the coin. And before you mock, it is more imperative today than ever. With the changing pace of technology, and those social networking sites people interact on, information spreads quicker than a bushfire. This role is not just keeping the coin, locking it away and forgetting about it. It requires diligence and attention to ensure the goddess's turtle remains safe.'

'I still don't understand what it is you do to protect the coin,' Nik said, scratching his head. 'As the saying goes "out of sight, out of mind". Isn't that the best way? If you can't see it, then no one can know about it.'

'If it were that simple.' Papou sighed. 'Many ancestors have tried to adopt that principle and failed. It is regrettable that flawed human behaviour impedes virtue.'

'What happens now? Do you need my decision right away?'

'I want you to take the time to think it over. You need to consider the expectations of this role. You cannot talk to anyone about what I told you today, nobody except me.'

'It's what you *haven't* said that troubles me,' Nik said.

'I can't tell you any more than what I have revealed, or the coin and you will be in danger.'

Nik swallowed, and asked, 'And if I decide not to take on the position of guardian, what happens then?'

Papou gazed across his backyard. 'The coin and I become inseparable.'

Nik blinked. 'What do you mean?'

His grandfather turned to him. 'What matters is that the coin remains hidden.'

Papou stood and started clearing the table. 'You have a lot to consider, Niko. If you become the coin's next guardian, your life will change.' He picked up the tray and looked at his grandson. 'The life of a protector isn't easy, but it has its rewards.'

Nik stared after his grandfather as he carried the tray into the house. His mind whirled and, after standing for a while, he picked up the empty beer bottles. He walked to the recycling bin and dropped them in. The bottles landed with a heavy thud and clinked as they hit against each other. He remained by the bin, motionless, holding the lid upright.

Could his grandfather have the onset of dementia? Had his mind conjured up this story? Papou didn't appear delusional and seemed to believe every word he spoke.

Nik dropped the lid and went into the house. He needed to research the symptoms of dementia and establish whether his grandfather showed signs of mental illness. Until he had more facts, he wouldn't mention any of this conversation to his parents. There was no point in having them worry if there was no need.

Nik rinsed his hands in the laundry and joined his grandfather, who was washing the dishes in the kitchen.

When he got home, Nik set his laptop on the low table in front of the lounge suite and searched for Alzheimer's disease. Hours later, he sat back and rubbed his tired eyes. From the various sources he'd read, Papou didn't show any of the indicators associated with the disease. Nik typed *Goddess's turtle* into a new tab and pressed the return button. Google spat out a list of links, but none referred to the coin. He entered another search term and learned that the Mesopotamians were the first ancient people to affix value to items by weight, and used silver rings as a system of currency, as early as 3100 BCE. Wanting more information, he checked another website and read that the first coins were introduced into the economy around the sixth or fifth century BCE. He kept reading until he saw a familiar name, his mouth dropping open.

His grandfather's words rang in his head as he re-read the opening lines of text:

Aphrodite was the first of Greek gods named and attributed to a coin. Her popularity amongst the ancient civilisations since prehistory shows her long affiliation with humans and of her importance in their lives.

He clicked on the hyperlink and a fresh page opened. There he saw the name Herodotos mentioned. He kept searching and clicked on a website on Aegina, displaying images of coins minted on the island. Nik leaned back on the sofa, his attention fastened on the graphic on the screen.

The old man wasn't senile.

Chapter Three

Nik woke up on the couch the next morning and sat up with a groan. His neck protested, the tendons tight as he stretched, moving his head from side to side. When he turned his head to the right, his eyes widened as he glimpsed the clock. 7:30 am. He bolted off the seat, swearing as he side-stepped the table and rushed towards the shower.

Forty minutes later he pulled in the school's car park and hurried to the cafeteria. Students called out in greeting as he entered the busy undercover area that provide shade during inclement weather and on hot days. He smiled and nodded at the boys, headed for the staff line and bought a vegemite roll.

'Late night, sir?' A few students called out as he walked past.

'More of a late start,' he said between mouthfuls of his roll.

'Sir? Sir?'

Nik turned. 'Good morning, Foster.' He waited until the four-teen-year-old reached him. 'What can I do for you?'

'Morning, sir. I, ah … I don't understand several questions in the assessment we're to hand in tomorrow.'

'And you waited until today to ask me?' Nik asked. The boy's face fell. 'Come to the library at lunchtime and I'll help you.'

'Thank you, sir!' The boy hurried back to his friends.

'And Foster!'

The boy skidded to a stop and turned. 'Sir?'

'Don't be late.'

'I won't, sir.'

The trip to his department's office took longer than he expected, with students stopping him along the way, wanting his attention. He placed his half-eaten roll, laptop, and case on the desk, picked up his mug and headed for the coffee jug.

'You look like shit, Nik,' said Harry, a colleague who was filling his cup with coffee. 'Big night, was it?'

'If only. Late one; researching.' Nik held out his cup, while Harry poured the strong aromatic brew. Nik took a sip and closed his eyes as he savoured the hot, bitter liquid.

'Must have been one heck of night "researching".' Harry raised his eyebrows and smirked.

'Maybe you can help? Do you know anything on the history of coins and mints?'

Harry stared at him, cup poised at his lips. 'Seriously? Is that what you were doing last night, researching coins?'

Nik nodded and took another sip of coffee.

'You need to get a life,' Harry said, shaking his head.

'I take that as a *no*.'

'You guessed right. Your best bet is to contact the numismatic society, someone there should be able to help.'

Nik raised his cup at Harry. 'That's a brilliant idea.'

The rest of the day passed by in a blur for Nik, his mind never far from his grandfather's revelation. After he dismissed his last class for the day, he sat down at the desk and looked up contact details for a local numismatic society. He clicked on a website and saw listings for clubs throughout the state. There was a name listed, a professor at Murdoch University, with an email address. He wrote the details down and then moved on to check more links. Minutes passed until he hit on the British Museum site.

According to the museum's records, the first coins came from Asia Minor, around the seventh century BCE, and then minting coins spread to the Greek world. Aegina was the earliest and busiest mint in Greece, one hundred years later. The more Nik read, more surprising facts came to light. Sicily had made silver coins during the same time. He clicked on a coin from Akragas, modern Agrigento. The image was impressive and detailed: on the obverse it had the sun-god Helios travelling on his chariot, an eagle flying overhead, and a crab below. On the reverse were two eagles standing on the body of a hare lying on a rock – one poised to tear into the flesh of the animal and the other, its head raised, screaming – and a grasshopper to the right.

Nik shut down his laptop. Information from the material he had searched and read last night and what he'd found now gave credence to part of the story told by his grandfather. The island of Aegina correlated with the history of the development and minting of coins, and the people worshipped Aphrodite over all other Greek gods. And he found images of turtles and the goddess's image etched onto steles, vases and kylixes displayed on websites, yet the information did not correlate to the goddess's coin, not the one his grandfather showed him. Although he hadn't expected to find much on it at all; its existence kept secret for centuries. He wanted to know more, such as how did his grandfather, and those protectors before him, keep the coin concealed for so long? And who were the other people his grandfather alluded to – those who must never learn of the coin's existence?

Nik gathered his belongings and left the classroom, locking the door behind him. He stretched his neck from side to side, grateful it was Friday and there would be no rushing around for the next two days.

'Yo, Nik! Coming up to the staffroom for drinks?' Harry called out.

'I'll be there in five!'

———————

THE STAFF common room got rowdier as teachers drifted in. Nik sat with two colleagues from his department and a few from the English department. He was chatting away with Christina about the lesson she was going to teach on Homer's *Iliad*, when someone tapped him on the shoulder.

'Hi there, Harry,' Nik said.

'How did you go with the coin people?' Harry turned to Christina. 'Young Nik here has a thing for coins.'

Nik ignored the dig. 'I found quite a few websites on coins, which is surprising.'

'Any of them useful?'

'As a matter of fact the British Museum had a lot of helpful information.'

Harry blinked. 'Ah … good.' He caught the attention of another teacher, mumbled an excuse and moved away.

'Is he always such a twat?' Christina asked, turning up her nose.

Nik shrugged. 'He has his moments.'

'What were you searching for?'

'Oh nothing much, I was just after information on ancient coins.'

'Did you find anything interesting?'

'I did, though how useful it will be, who knows,' he replied smiling. 'Sometimes it's handy to store inane facts.' He tapped his head with a finger.

'I don't believe learning new content is worthless,' she commented.

Nik gave her a slight smile and drained the rest of his beer. 'Would you like another glass of wine? I'm getting another drink.'

'I will, thank you.' Christina reached for her bag.

'That's fine, I'll get it.' He took her glass and stood. As he walked away, he noticed one of the female English teachers lean across to speak to Christina. Nik knew of the interest the single female staff had in him and, although they were nice to talk to, none of them attracted him. His mother despaired at his single status, but Nik didn't want to be with a woman to satisfy his family's desire for a daughter-in-law, and he felt it was unfair to lead someone into a relationship with no future. He wanted a permanent and long-lasting partnership, like his grandparents' and his parents'. He stayed another hour before he said his goodbyes and left for his parents' place.

When he arrived, Nik let himself into the house and headed straight for the kitchen, where he found his mother putting a dish in the oven.

'Hi, Mum.' He kissed her on the cheek.

'Nik, you look tired,' she said, as she pushed a strand of dark wavy hair from her face. With her olive complexion, green eyes, and statuesque body, she was an attractive woman and always smiling.

'Busy day at work,' he said, as he reached for an olive from the jar sitting on the kitchen bench and popped it into his mouth. His mother slapped his hand.

'Make yourself helpful and scoop some into that bowl.' She handed him a small ladle. 'How are those boys treating you at school?'

Nik shrugged. 'They're fine. No different from when I was growing up.'

'Now you get a taste of your own medicine,' she said with a laugh.

Nik chuckled. 'At least I know what to expect.' He placed the bowl filled with olives on a platter next to the prepared cheeses and grabbed a piece. 'Besides, some teachers I had were boring, didn't change the way they taught the curriculum, while others were brilliant and innovative, and incorporated interactive strategies to engage us in the learning. That's what I do in my classes.'

'Your students may think that is boring to them.' She waved a pair of silver tongs at him. 'No matter what, students believe their teachers are dull, even today with all that fancy technology you use.'

'That's possible, but not true. My lessons are always interesting and the students enjoy them,' Nik said, grinning. 'How was your day at the surgery? Did old Mrs Kosta come and see you?'

His mother worked at a practice where a lot of migrants, not just Greeks, went to see her. Mrs Kosta lived a few houses down from his grandfather's place and knew the family from the day his grandparents moved into the street. He watched his mother pile the platter with cured ham, Italian salamis, crusty bread and pickled dill.

'Poor dear, she wants a little attention. No harm in that.'

Nik raised a brow. 'Isn't that the case with all your patients? I'm sure many of them make appointments so they can complain about their families and gossip.'

'Don't be cheeky. They are lonely and many cannot speak English. They want to talk to someone who understands them.'

'Hmm … And how many of your appointments are patients who are sick?'

'Ah Nik, it's not as black and white as you think.'

'You're too soft, Mum,' he said with a fond smile. 'Who's all this food for? I thought it was just me tonight?'

'Niko,' greeted his father, stepping into the kitchen.

Nik turned. 'Hi Dad, how are you?'

'Good.' His father was tall and lean, shoulders slightly curved, with thick black hair and a face etched with deep lines. The years of drug abuse made him look much older than his age. 'A beer?'

'Sure.'

His father opened the refrigerator and grabbed two stubbies. He turned to his wife. 'A glass of wine, my darling?'

'Yes, my sweet.' She smiled at him, and Nik turned away, rolling his eyes.

'Your sister is bringing a friend to dinner,' she told Nik.

'Is Chara bringing her new bloke?' asked his father, eyes gleaming.

'Yes, and be nice to him,' his mother said in a firm voice.

'Of course.' The corner of his father's eyes crinkled with mischief. Nik hid a smile and took a mouthful of beer.

'Your mother told me Papou left you a cryptic message yesterday? He did always have a flair for the dramatic.'

'Leon,' his mother lowered her voice.

His father shrugged, his expression bitter. 'Did you find out what he wanted?'

Nik nodded. 'He wants to go over old family records, and for me to help him.'

'Ridiculous! He can do that on his own now he's retired. He has plenty of time,' Leon growled.

'I haven't said yes,' said Nik.

'Good!'

'Nik is a historian, he may find it interesting to learn of the family's heritage,' his mother pointed out. 'Besides, your mother was a beautiful woman and it would be nice for Nik to hear more about her.'

Leon's face mellowed at the mention of his mother. 'She was kind, generous hearted, and way too good for the old man.'

'Your father loved her very much.'

'Yes, well …'

'Help me fix the table,' she ordered. 'Chara and James will be here soon.'

Chapter Four

On Saturday morning, Nik drove to the farmers' market and stocked up for the week on locally grown vegetables, fruit and organic meat. He bought fresh bread and rolls from an artisan bakery and made his way home. A few hours later he rang his grandfather.

'Niko! Good morning, how are you?'

'Hi Papou, I'm fine. And you?'

'Good, good.'

They both fell silent.

'Are you home today?' Nik asked, breaking the lengthy pause.

'I am home now but going out later this afternoon.'

'Oh.'

'Why don't you come now and we'll eat lunch together?'

'Okay. I'll be there soon. What can I bring?'

'A nice bottle of red wine would be good.'

'No worries, I'll see you in a little while.'

Fifty minutes later, Nik and his grandfather sat in the kitchen, each with a glass of red wine, and the table laden with various cuts of cured meats, cheese, olives, bread, sliced tomato and lettuce.

'I need to understand why you chose now to tell me about the role of the guardianship,' said Nik.

'I had to wait until you were ready to accept responsibility,' Papou said. 'There is no handbook and each successor, whoever he or she is, show their readiness to fulfil their duty at different ages, some as young as seventeen, and others much later, not until their thirties.'

'So I'm a late bloomer?'

Iasos shook his head. 'Thirty is a suitable age, mature, youthful and strong, both mentally and physically, to accept the role as guardian.'

'There have been female protectors?'

'Oh yes, the first guardian was a woman.'

Nik stared at his grandfather, digesting this latest piece of news.

'She was the reason the coin remained concealed and written out of history.'

'Who was she?' Nik asked.

Papou tapped his nose with a finger. 'Only the keepers may know.'

Nik studied his grandfather for a moment. 'I read that the first proper coins came from Asia Minor in the seventh century BCE, then a hundred years later, the Greeks learned the procedure of minting coins. Centuries before that, the Mesopotamians introduced the concept of exchanging legal tender for goods.'

The sides of Papou's mouth lifted into a slight curve. 'You've gone to the effort to do a little research.'

'There's nothing on the coin you showed me but I found a few similar examples.'

'And that is it. You'll find no further information on it.'

'Then how is it these others you mentioned are aware of the coin?'

'For as long as guardians existed, there coexisted a small group of people who coveted the coin. Many tried to seize it, and individuals died protecting the coin.'

'*If* I take on the role, what's the next step?' asked Nik.

'We begin your training.' Papou leaned over and placed a hand on Nik's. 'My dear boy, if you agree to be my successor, no-one, not your parents, friends, or girlfriend, can ever learn what I tell you, or what you must do.'

'I don't have a girlfriend,' he said.

Papou patted his hand and smiled. 'There is time ... the right woman will appear when you least expect it and render you senseless.'

'Is that how it happened when you met Yiayiá?'

Still smiling, his grandfather sat back and nodded. 'It was the best moment in my life, the first time I saw her, and the second when she agreed to marry me.' He took a sip of his wine.

Nik peered into his wineglass, the burgundy liquid mesmerising as his thoughts ping-ponged from one subject to the next. 'What is the likelihood there's a current threat to steal the coin?'

Papou shrugged. 'There is always the possibility. That is why it is important to protect the coin.'

'Did you encounter any problems?'

'The difficulties for one guardian to the next are different. Some were negligible while others experienced challenges.'

Nik shook his head. A wry smile crept across his face. 'That's not an answer.'

'It's the explanation you'll get.'

'Right ... only the keeper will be told everything.'

'Exactly.'

Nik eyeballed his grandfather, torn between wanting to hear more and equally uncertain that he wanted to know. His grandfather sat relaxed, the years of experience and knowledge etched on his wizened face. Nik's left knee bounced up and down as he tried to read his grandfather's laconic expression.

He drew in a deep breath. 'I will do it. I will be the coin's next guardian.'

'You have made an old man overjoyed and proud.' Papou beamed, reached for the wine bottle and topped up the glasses. 'Here's to you, the newest protector of the goddess's turtle.' Papou raised his glass in a toast.

Nik squelched down the butterflies in his stomach, both excited and hesitant at the prospect of his new role. He was eager to learn more of the coin's and his ancestors' history, though he doubted there was anything sinister or dangerous to being a guardian. The coin appeared to be harmless. Besides its priceless value, he couldn't understand the need for secrecy.

'When do we start?' he asked.

'Tomorrow. Now let's enjoy the food.'

Nik reached for a bread roll, split it in half and filled it with the cured meat, cheese, sliced tomato and lettuce. He took a bite and glanced at his grandfather, busy filling his roll.

'Who was the original owner of the coin?'

'Herakles.' Papou bit into his roll, not fazed by Nik's gobsmacked expression.

'No way! He existed?'

'He did.'

'I thought the legend of Herakles was to do with remedying wrongs, a moralistic analogy?'

'It is, but the story didn't come out of nowhere. Myths developed from the acts and deeds of actual people. How else do you think they originated?' Papou took another bite.

'Does that mean the Bible ...' Nik couldn't finish the sentence.

'To a certain extent. A lot of the stories came from ancient oral traditions and over the ages were reinterpreted and rewritten to suit the propaganda of the time.'

Nik put his roll on the plate, grabbed his glass and gulped the rest of the peppery wine.

'Homer's *Iliad*?'

'You've been to Mykenai and Troy. What do you think?'

Nik's mind whirled. He needed to digest what his grandfather had divulged. The mythologies were devised from actual events and people? Was that difficult to conceive? He imagined in a hundred years, or a thousand, people could say the same for what had transpired in the past two centuries.

'I don't know, Papou. It sounds far-fetched, even for you,' he said. 'Mythologies originated to teach illiterate people the outcome of decisions and deeds. Besides being significant stories, they were a guidebook on how to live an honourable life.'

'They were,' Papou agreed, 'and still continue to be valid to this day. As we begin your education, I will challenge your beliefs and perspective of the world. You will question the validity of what you will see, read and hear. But, as they say, "the truth is stranger than fiction".'

'How could Herakles own a coin when, according to historical sources, the first one originated in the seventh century? The legend of Herakles goes back further, before the invention of currency.'

'That is the official date given by scholars. The goddess's turtle came from the isle of Aegina,' Papou answered.

'I don't get it,' Nik said. 'It wasn't possible for Herakles to own the coin when it didn't even exist in his time.'

'As you will soon learn, nothing is impossible or improbable,' his grandfather said, his eyes twinkling.

Nik felt exasperated. 'This is frustrating, Papou! You're not answering my questions.'

'As I said earlier, we start tomorrow. Come by at six.'

'Why the late start?'

'Six a.m., my boy. I'll have a schedule drawn up with what we'll cover.'

'I was hoping for a sleep-in,' Nik said with a grumble.

'Wear your exercise gear.'

'So much for a day of rest.' He took a bite of his roll, studied his grandfather for a moment. 'Why now?'

'Why now what?'

'Why are you asking me to take over the guardianship of the coin now?' asked Nik.

His grandfather swallowed and then reached for the wine, taking a sip. As he set the glass down, he wiped his mouth with a napkin. 'There comes a time in a guardian's life when the decision to induct a new protector must take precedence over one's desire to remain the sole custodian or before one's demise. My father wasn't able to complete my training before going to war. I learnt much of the role from reading logs and diaries from those who preceded my father and grandfather. I did not want that to happen to my successor.'

Chapter Five

There was a slight chill in the air when Nik stepped outside, the red-orange glow of the sun announcing a fresh day. He yawned as he unlocked the car, threw his bag with a change of clothes onto the back seat and got behind the wheel.

When he arrived at his grandfather's house, Papou was waiting in the driveway.

'Morning, Papou,' said Nik, as his grandfather opened the passenger door and got in. 'I take it we're heading somewhere.'

'Good morning.' Papou strapped himself in. 'We're going to Perry Lakes Stadium.'

Nik put the car in reverse and backed out of the driveway. 'They wouldn't be open at this hour, not on a Sunday.'

'I have a key.'

'How is it you have the key?'

'The person in charge of maintenance and I are old friends. I used to go there to run on the tracks.'

'Is that what I'm going to be doing? Running?'

'To start with.'

The roads were quiet with minimal traffic as they headed west towards the old stadium. It didn't take long to reach their destination. Nik was saddened to see how rundown the place was, yet it had been the finest complex in the 1960s, when Perth hosted the Commonwealth Games.

'I thought the council sold the place,' he said as he turned onto the road heading to the arena.

'It has been sold,' Papou acknowledged. 'The contractors start demolition soon. My friend will let me know when that will happen.'

Nik stopped the car, the way ahead gated. His grandfather got out and unlocked the gate. He waved Nik through and closed it before getting back in the car. Nik pulled up behind the old grandstand and turned off the engine, and followed his grandfather as he led the way onto the running track.

'A few stretches to warm up those muscles and then I want you to run the circuit,' said Papou.

'Been a while since I've run the whole track.' Nik clasped the back of his neck. 'What if I start with one hundred metres?'

'The whole four hundred metres.'

'Right.'

Nik stretched his legs with a variety of exercises and started around the track at a jog. He wasn't sure how a workout would help to be a guardian of a tiny object. The adage 'a sound mind in a healthy body' popped into his head. Perhaps there was something to it. The ancient Greeks understood it was important: the two worked in harmony when in good physical condition. And the Romans followed in their stead. His grandfather was the epitome of fitness; many people his age did not look as good as he did.

Even at a jog, Nik's breathing sounded harsh to his ears. His lungs struggled to draw in air. Sweat trickled down his face and his singlet clung to his torso. As he approached the spot where his grandfather stood, he could see the frown on Papou's face. Nik came to a lurching stop, hands on hips and breathing hard.

'I didn't realise how unfit you are.' His grandfather squinted at him. 'Don't you work out?'

'I ... do,' Nik answered, puffing. 'Weights ... occasional run ...... on a treadmill.'

'Do you swim?'

'Sometimes.'

'Right. Okay, got your breath back?'

Nik nodded.

'Time for the one hundred metre sprint. See that marker?' Papou pointed.

'Yes.'

'You run there and back.'

Nik moved a few steps away and waited for his grandfather.

'Off you go.'

Nik took off. When he returned, his grandfather told him to go again. Back and forth he went until told to stop. His grandfather gave him a bottle of water. Nik drank half in one gulp. Before his body got too cool, he stretched his limbs. His leg shook as he pulled the other up for a quad stretch.

'Is this necessary?' he asked, wiping the sweat from his forehead.

'I must prepare you for every contingency, plus it is healthy for you,' replied his grandfather.

'Still, it's just a coin.'

'You'll soon learn there's more to being a guardian, and why.' Papou handed him a towel. 'We'll head home for breakfast and I'll go over the schedule with you.'

When they arrived, Nik headed for the shower while his grandfather prepared food.

'Hmmm ... that smells good,' Nik said fifteen minutes later, walking into the kitchen.

'Here you go.' Papou placed a plate and a Greek coffee on the table in front of him.

Nik picked up the fork and knife and cut into his bacon. His grandfather sat down with a smaller serving, reached for a manila folder and handed it to him. Nik flipped it open and scanned the pages, ten in total. He stopped chewing as he turned each page. He returned to the beginning and read through again. When finished, he looked up at Papou, who had watched him in silence.

'I'm surprised you allowed me time to eat and sleep,' Nik quipped. 'In all seriousness, Papou, you can't expect me to follow such a gruelling schedule. I need to teach, I have marking to do and co-curricular activities to run.'

'The first few months are intense,' said Papou. 'But it will ease once you have mastered the skills. When the first person discovered that the coin had unusual properties, it became the guardians' duty to develop strategies to protect it.'

Nik glanced at the typed sheets of paper. 'This looks extreme, though. Running, weights and weapons training, boxing, martial arts, and sources to read and research, plus the sessions with you. This could be the program for the ancient Olympic Games.' He flicked through the typed pages as he re-read the sections. 'If the coin is this dangerous, why hasn't someone destroyed it, or locked away it in a vault?'

'A good question, one I asked my father when he started my training,' Papou replied. 'And I will give you the same answer he gave me, "The coin is our link to history, both familial and the world. It binds us as it is bound to us. One without the other cannot exist."'

Nik frowned. 'Are you saying we're connected to the coin? We're here because of it?'

Papou gave a hesitant nod. 'In a fashion. It evolved because of an event which led to a decision that tied our bloodline to the coin.'

'What do you mean?'

'Before we jump too far ahead, you need to learn how our family got involved. Have you finished?' Papou pointed to his half full plate. 'I want to show you something.'

Nik scoffed down the now cold, congealed egg, bacon and sausage. Papou had risen and taken his plate to the sink bowl. Nik put his on top.

'Leave those, I'll do them later. Come with me,' said Papou.

Nik followed his grandfather along the passageway and into the bathroom. He opened his mouth to ask a question when Papou leaned over the tub, grabbed the spout and turned it anti-clockwise.

'Holy shit!' Nik jumped back.

The pink enamel tub groaned and squeaked as it swung away from the wall, coming to a stop at a forty-five-degree angle, to reveal a passage in the floor. A set of stairs led downwards, and lights winked on one by one to reveal a steel door at the bottom. Papou marched down the staircase and turned when he reached the door. His eyes twinkled at Nik's stunned expression.

Nik peered under the tub. 'What about the plumbing?' he asked. He looked from the bathtub to the vast hole in the floor, unable to comprehend what he was seeing. It was like a scene from the old 1960s *Get Smart* series, and the weird contraptions and inventions underpinning the secret agency and its goofball agent.

'The plumber set the taps and faucet in the wall to avoid jeopardising the water pipes, and rerouted the drainage system,' his grandfather told him. 'The next enormous job was setting steel tracks and large ball bearings into the floor to move the bathtub.'

Papou beckoned him. 'But what I need to show you is in here.' He tapped at a panel on the wall, there was a click and the heavy door swung open. Lights flickered beyond him.

Nik took a hesitant step and with faltering movements made his way down. As soon as he stepped onto the landing, his grandfather pressed a button near the light switch. Nik whipped his head around to see the bathtub had shifted back into place and the lights dimmed on the stairway.

Papou opened the door further and entered the room. With a

halting step, Nik crossed the threshold. As he did so, his mouth fell open. On the wall to his left was a bank of television monitors, streaming live images of various places. Three computers sat below, their monitors glowing and running programs. To his right stood wall-to-ceiling bookshelves, much like a high Victorian library, with a ladder to get to the top shelf. In the middle of the room was a large, blue exercise mat, the size of a boxing ring. On the far wall, locked in wooden cabinets, was an array of weapons: swords, shields, guns, rifles, bow and quiver full of arrows, spears, daggers, and a kevlar vest. It was a collection of weaponry from throughout the ages.

'Oh … my … god!' Nik could not believe his eyes. He didn't know what to think. 'How long has this been here?'

'Since I became the next keeper,' his grandfather replied.

'And how many years is that?' Nik walked over to the monitors.

'Near sixty years now. Before he went to war, my father told me how the coin was now my responsibility. He wanted to make sure there was a successor in place, in case he didn't return. He made it back home but died shortly afterwards.'

'You were, what … twenty-something years old when you became guardian? So young.'

'Younger. I was in my teens when my father left for the war.'

'I need to sit.'

Nik dropped himself into the nearest computer chair. He glanced around the room again, still struggling to absorb what he was seeing.

'The room has changed over the years, in particular the technology as it got better and faster, but technical advances cannot replace certain objects with bits and bytes.' Papou strode over to the bookshelf and placed a loving hand on the books. 'Many of these editions date back over hundreds of years, and there are several thousands of years old. I store those in an airtight and secure room.'

'Thousands of years?' Nik repeated. He glanced across to the weapons. 'Even those?'

Papou smiled. 'Those are my prized possessions.' He walked to the furthest cabinet. 'These belonged to the earliest guardians, dating back to 1500 BCE, and were used during the Trojan War.'

Nik's grandfather said something else, but Nik didn't hear him speak: he felt dizzy. The room swam and his body felt hot and cold. Little bright stars filled his vision. He slipped from the chair, his limbs jelly-like. The last thing he saw was his grandfather rush towards him.

When he woke he was lying on the blue mat, a cold compress over his forehead. His grandfather was sitting nearby with a worried expression on his face. Nik propped himself up on an elbow, the face cloth falling onto the mat.

'What happened?'

'You fainted.'

'What? I did not. I've never fainted! Ever!'

'Okay, you passed out,' Papou said with concern. 'Maybe seeing this room and hearing about the items is too much. Perhaps you are not ready to take on the position.'

'I'll admit it came as a bit of a shock. I was expecting … Well, I'm not sure what.'

'Hmm. I am going too fast for you,' Papou said, his brows knitted, 'too much information too soon.'

'No, no,' said Nik, shaking his head. 'I think it's the realisation of the responsibility. This room and the contents took me by surprise. I imagined nothing of this magnitude.'

'Regardless, we progress slower,' Papou said, as he stood. 'I don't want you to feel burdened or pressured.' Papou shook his head, angry at himself. 'I am such a fool. I was excited about sharing our family's legacy with you and forgot to check how you were coping.'

Nik scrambled to his feet. 'I want to be the keeper and I'm ready. A minor glitch, that's all. It won't happen again.'

Papou studied him, his light blue eyes searching. 'I don't know, Niko. It is a unique world with a huge obligation. It's not just the coin's secret you are protecting, it's all of this too.'

'I am prepared and committed.' Nik stood firm with determination. 'I want to learn everything. I am the next keeper of the goddess's turtle.'

Nik nursed the cup of coffee Papou had made for him in the kitchenette recessed behind the door. Two worn but comfortable lounge chairs, and a low rectangular wooden table, the glossy surface long gone, faced the bookshelf. They both sat on the chairs. Nik scanned the titles of the books on the shelves. He itched to peruse the books; many in the collection were rare editions.

'How could Herakles own the coin before the Greeks invented minting?' he asked. The thought had been bothering him since the previous day.

'What he had was a nugget, no bigger than a quail's egg.'

'So how did he come into possession of the rock?'

'Some said he picked it up during one of his deeds, others assumed his father, Zeus, gave it to him. A few were of the opinion he stole it from a miner who was bragging about a substantial find he discovered,' said Papou. 'I suspect he pocketed it. He was a bit of a rogue and had no qualms in procuring items he wanted. Besides, it was a good-sized rock to use in a slingshot.'

'That's not how he's portrayed in the myths.'

'He completed extraordinary deeds and people loved to hear the stories.'

'What I don't get is it's just a coin, priceless yes, but why the secrecy?'

'I will explain. Herakles, while out on a hunt, took down a deer with his sling, as he fancied himself as quite the marksman. In his haste, he fumbled with the stones and dropped them. Later he decided no one should ever learn of the nugget's power and protected it at all costs.'

'Wait a minute, what happened when he dropped the rocks?'

'He did not tell a soul of his experience. When he passed the nugget on to his son, he told him never to touch the stone but to keep it secured in a pouch and hidden. Each descendant thereafter was given the same instruction, and every guardian since stayed faithful to Herakles' wishes. But when Helen of Sparta received the nugget, it was the most dangerous time in all the world's history.'

'You're kidding! *The* Helen, Homer's Helen? She existed?'

'Niko, you will soon learn that the truth between fact and fiction is much more blurred than you realise,' said Papou.

'Helen of Troy,' Nik said in wonder. He sat back, eyes wide, then jerked his head towards his grandfather, thunderstruck. 'Helen was … we're … she's our ancestor?' He blinked. 'Wait! That means Herakles was as well!'

'She wasn't his blood relative, though the ties between Tyndareus, Helen's father, and Herakles were close. Herakles had killed the king of Sparta, Hippocoon, and his sons, who took part in the death of his uncle. He entrusted Tyndareus with ruling the region. But, no, we're not of her bloodline.'

'Oh.' Nik was disappointed. 'So how did she end up with the nugget?'

'Years later, Herakles' children were seeking refuge and went to Sparta, knowing Tyndareus would provide shelter. Hyllos, the eldest of Herakles' children, beguiled by the young Helen who, in exchange for a kiss, gave her the most precious item he owned when she asked for a gift. He gave her the stone.'

'He gave it to her?' asked Nik, incredulous.

Papou nodded. 'Even as a young girl Helen was beautiful and precocious. She knew how to beguile and seduce even the wiliest of men, and always got what she wanted.'

'What an idiot.' Nik shook his head. 'And no doubt he told her what the stone could do.'

'He did, and stressed the importance of not telling anyone of its existence.'

'All for a kiss? How stupid can one be?'

'This was Helen,' Papou pointed out. 'No man could deny her and she was very desirable.'

Nik snorted. 'Evidently Hyllos wasn't thinking with his brain!'

Papou chuckled. 'I am sure you've been in situations where lust overruled your brain.'

Nik's cheeks warmed. 'Well, I wouldn't give away a valuable object for a pretty face.'

Papou shook his finger at him. 'Don't make such statements you cannot guarantee to fulfil. Even the most stalwart of us are putty in a woman's hands.'

'What happened after Hyllos gave Helen the nugget? Did she heed his warning?'

'She did and, not only that, she made sure no one in her family or her attendants learned of its existence.'

A chill snaked up Nik's spine. 'She had it with her while she was at Ilios.' It was more a statement than a question.

Papou's expression gave the answer.

'Cripes! She worked out what it did and used it,' said Nik, aghast.

'Nope. Helen kept her word to Hyllos. She never discovered the properties of the stone and kept it hidden during the ten years the city was under siege.' Papou stood. 'Another coffee?'

Nik nodded and handed over his cup. He had to readjust his

view of the woman for whom legions of men had died. Though the war the Greeks declared on the Trojans had a more sinister agenda: power and greed.

Papou returned with two steaming cups of brewed coffee, the rich mouth-watering aroma filling the otherwise sterile room. Nik sipped the smooth, dark liquid and closed his eyes.

'Good?' asked Papou, with a slight grin on his face.

Nik looked at him with a crooked smile. 'Very.' He crossed his legs. 'What's the story with the sword and shield?'

'Our ancestor fought in the war, and was among the few lucky ones to return home. He was a Spartan and on the same ship as Helen and Menelaos.'

'Is that how the role of keeper started?'

'No, he became Helen's bodyguard.' Papou placed his cup on the table, and stood and walked to the bookshelf. He plucked a book, sat back on the chair and held it out. The book was old, the cover made from cloth, the title written in Greek.

'I've read this,' said Nik, scanning the cover.

'Not this version. Take it home. This is as close to the original story as we will ever get. When Homer sang the events of the war, he merged several historical battles in one dramatic epic. The transcription of this publication originated from the first printed source of the *Iliad*. The ones that followed were copied from later adaptations, of which numerous passages were misinterpreted.'

'Is this the first edition of the *Iliad*?' Nik gaped at the book in his hands. 'I can't take it home.' He thrust the book back at his grandfather. 'I wouldn't be able to live with myself if something happened to it. I will read it here and nowhere else.'

Papou took the book. 'If that's what you prefer.'

Nik sighed in relief, his hands dropping onto his lap. 'I do, and if it's okay with you, I'll come here and read the books you suggest.'

'That is fine. I thought you would like to read in the comfort of your own home.'

'Any other book I would, but considering the age and how rare the collection is, I'd feel more comfortable reading here.' Nik rubbed his hands up and down his thighs a few times and then clasped them together. 'Going back to Helen, she was the first official guardian of the stone?'

'Yes, she was,' Papou replied.

'Then how did our family become the protector of the coin if we're not related to Helen?'

'Following Helen's return to Sparta, Menelaos assigned a warrior to guard her at all times. The king tasked our ancestor to protect her.'

Nik sat up straighter in his chair. 'Our predecessor's first gig was as a bodyguard to the keeper? Did he know about the object she safeguarded?'

'Guarding Helen was his priority and thereafter, the two families were bound by that initial position. Helen's descendants not once divulged the treasure they possessed. Later, unfortunate circumstances saw Helen's royal line cease and new laws introduced into Sparta. It changed the city-state and with it, the most extreme living conditions.'

'What happened to the nugget?'

'Remember Hyllos, Herakles' son?'

Nik nodded. He leaned forward, elbows on his knees, and waited for Papou to continue.

'He and his siblings left Sparta a few years later and settled in Athens. Eurystheus, the king of Mykenai, wanted Herakles' sons to answer for the murder of a king, but the Athenians refused to give them up and war ensued. Hyllos killed Eurystheus, hacked off his head and presented it to his grandmother, Herakles' mother, who gouged out the king's eyes with weaving pins.'

'A lot of anger there,' said Nik.

'Not long after, Hyllos and his brothers decided they wanted to reclaim the Peloponnese, following their paternal grandfather's footsteps, Perseus, who founded Mykenai, and invaded the region.

Hyllos also wanted to retrieve the stone from Helen, realising he made a mistake in giving it to her. It didn't go well, and the Mykenaians killed Hyllos. Decades later, the third Heraklide generation attacked and conquered southern Greece. As for the stone, Herakles' descendants searched and questioned every person in Sparta, but no-one had heard of or seen it. One of Helen's ancestors had given the nugget to the bodyguard, told him to leave Sparta and return "when two kings, one of them a lion", was born.'

'What an odd thing to say.'

'Not at all,' said Papou, with a firm shake of his head. 'You must remember people in that period consulted the oracle at Delphi in times of crises, and to seek answers. Helen's descendant did the same and followed the advice given.'

'Where did he go?'

'To the island of Aegina.'

'Home of the first mint,' said Nik in a rush, the pieces of the puzzle fitting together.

'Yes.' Papou nodded. 'He settled there and had a family, and each new generation was given specific instructions. The stone was later smelted and turned into a coin. There was enough material to make two. The mould and refuse were later collected and destroyed by the guardian.'

'How?'

'That secret died with the one who commissioned the coin.'

'Where's the second coin?'

'That is a mystery, and I have spent decades trying to learn what happened to it. The coins remained together for three hundred years, until one disappeared with this lion king. Or at least that's the assumption. However, there is no evidence of the second coin. It is like it never existed. But it did, for knowledge of it is a part of our historical records.'

'What do you think happened to it?' asked Nik.

'Someone who knew of the coins took it from the king when he was slain in battle.'

'If the guardians kept the coins hush-hush, how could anyone else know of them? Did the king blurt it out during a drunken evening, or an ancestor blabbed?'

'The king entrusted with the coins did not drink, Spartan law forbade its citizens from drinking alcohol. As to an ancestor being the culprit, that is not a possibility.'

'How can you be sure an ancestor didn't blab or brag about the coin?' asked Nik. 'Even the most level-headed person, if enticed, may give up any secret, just as you said earlier, when Hyllos gave up the stone for a kiss from Helen.'

'It's more probable someone overheard the king and his body-guard discussing the coins and the impending combat.' Papou got up and walked over to the weapons cabinet. He touched the wall to the left of it, or so Nik thought, and a small panel hissed open. His grandfather typed in a code and a door swung ajar. Nik joined him. 'This cuirass, helmet, greaves, shield and sword belonged to King Leonidas. He instructed his bodyguard to strip his body should he die.'

Nik stared at the golden body armour and black-plumed helmet. Apart from many dents, both shone like new. The bronze casing of the hoplite shield gleamed under the fluorescent light, emphasising the pockmarks and cuts etched into the surface. The iron blade of the sword told a story of many battles, with nicks bitten into the edge, and the hilt darkened from sweat and blood. The hair at Nik's nape stood on end when he looked at the next weapon.

'That would inflict nasty wounds.'

'It did. This was the Spartans' preferred weapon of choice.' Papou reached across and grabbed the short thick sword with its curved blade. 'It's called a *Kopis,* and it's used for hacking, much like an axe. See this?' Papou held the sword at the neck of the blade with one hand and rested the length on the palm of his other. 'An ingenious design, contoured to the grip of the hand,

and the curved tail made it less likely for the warrior to drop it during a fight.' He held it out to Nik. 'Here, take it.'

Nik grabbed the handle and when his grandfather let go, the blade swung downwards. He had to use both hands to lift it.

He bit his bottom lip. 'This is heavier than it looks. How did they ever swing it, let alone use it in battle?' The muscles in his upper arms tightened as he struggled to hold the sword upright.

'Years of training,' said Papou, retrieving the sword. He placed it back into its niche, pressed a button on the panel and the cabinet swung close.

'This room is like a museum, the way you've organised it, and with the air-locked environment,' Nik commented as they returned to the chairs.

'One of the major roles of a guardian is to preserve the artefacts, and ensure we do not damage them,' stated Papou. 'It is important to maintain them, and learn their history so you can teach the next successor.'

'It must have taken decades to learn everything here,' Nik said, staggered. 'Just these books alone would take a lifetime to read.'

'I hope you have a lifetime,' said Papou. 'The paramount matter is to prioritise.' He pointed to the computers. 'I've set up the computers to search for particular terms relating to the goddess's coin, including for the words tortoise, Aphrodite, travelling, Herodotos, Herakles, anything related to the history of the coin, including Hitler and his followers, plus certain locations. Anything that turns up will need revising depending on the pingbacks and where they are. Before computers it was harder to track any queries about the coin, and required a lot of time reading international newspapers, listening to the radio stations of other nations, connecting with experts and sometimes piggybacking on law enforcement networks and government agencies. These days it is easier to search, but the volume is so much greater. You must verify and validate the information with the resources here and online, and when you cannot source the material you need, ask the experts.'

'Really? Is that safe? Won't the people I contact ask questions?' asked Nik.

'I have found people are happy to share information if you are querying academic theories, or asking for advice.' Papou tapped his nose. 'You show an interest in their work and they will talk and show their life's research.'

'I'll keep that in mind.' Nik stretched out his legs. 'But back to King Leonidas. I read few Spartans survived the battle of Thermopylae. From what I understand, any Spartan warriors who returned home are those who didn't fight well or were injured, and were treated like lepers and vilified.'

'That's true.' Papou attested. 'However, King Leonidas told his bodyguard not to return to Sparta.'

'Is that when our ancestors became the guardians of the coin?'

Papou shook his head. 'The king wanted the coin to go to the descendant of Odysseus.'

'Ithaka! We have family there?'

'Yes. The bodyguard settled on the island, married a local girl and had an extensive family. His descendants are now scattered across mainland Greece. And then there's us, here in Australia. That's enough for today, I don't want to overwhelm you with too much in one day.'

'I'm fine. I want to hear more.'

'I'm glad you do but let's leave it until next weekend.'

'What? That's way too long to wait.'

'We'll train during the week, and on the weekend we'll resume the history lesson,' said Papou. 'Besides, don't you have work to do?'

Nik scrunched up his nose. 'I should prep lessons for the week and mark the Year 12 papers. They'll want to know their results.' He stood, picked up the empty coffee cups, and took them to the sink to wash.

Chapter Seven
____

Each morning at five o'clock, Nik picked up his grandfather and drove to Perry Lakes for laps and sprints. Afterwards he drove back to shower and eat breakfast at his grandfather's, then on to school for a full day of teaching. He worked out at the gym for an hour of weight training after school, then went home for dinner, marking, and watched a bit of television to relax before bed.

On the eighth Saturday morning, Nik groaned when his alarm chimed. He threw off the bedcovers and stumbled his way to the wardrobe, pulling out clean running shorts and a singlet. He shuffled into the bathroom, washed his face with chilly water and rinsed out his mouth. Yawning, he returned to the bedroom, grabbed a pair of socks and picked up his exercise bag filled with clean clothes he had packed the previous night. On his way out he stopped by the kitchen, filled up a water bottle and a glass, which he downed in a few gulps.

The street lights were still on as he drove the familiar route to his grandfather's. Papou was waiting on the footpath, as he had done for the past two months. Nik pulled up alongside and slipped the gearshift into neutral. His grandfather opened the door but didn't get in.

'Park in the driveway, Niko, we're doing something different this morning.' He shut the door and walked back to the porch and waited for Nik.

'Why aren't we going to the track?' Nik asked as he joined his grandfather.

'I will introduce you to weapons and defence training,' said Papou, pulling the fly-screen door open.

'I've nothing against learning how to defend myself, but why weapons? I don't see the relevance,' Nik said as he followed his grandfather into the bathroom. 'It's a coin, not a person.'

'I asked my father the same question, and I will give you the answer he gave me: "Being prepared, no matter the circumstance or the purpose, gives you the skills to rationalise with clarity." My father believed there was a potential threat, and we were not the only ones aware of the coin's existence. He did not know when others would learn or hear about the coin, but he was convinced it would happen. Having the coin in my care all this time, I agree with my father's assessment.'

'In the time of your guardianship, did you encounter any problems or witness signs other people were seeking the coin?' Nik queried. His grandfather walked down the steps and paused at the steel door. He looked up at Nik.

'The question you should ask is, "Who wants the coin and what is their intent?"'

'Do you believe people are looking for it?'

'I spent my life dedicated to protecting the coin, as those before me have done. For thousands of years our family sacrificed their lives and service to ensure the coin remains a secret. What do you think?' Papou's eyes darkened.

Nik lowered his head and shuffled his feet. 'It seems too far-fetched to be true; somewhat like those adventure books or Indiana Jones movies.'

'Where do you suppose the stories came from?' said Papou with a snort. 'Actual events inspired the authors and bards, how else could Homer concoct such a tale?'

'I guess the notion of a rare coin possessing inexplicable qualities is difficult to accept. Besides, this stuff doesn't happen to ordinary people. I'm a teacher, nothing more.'

'I was a teacher,' Papou pointed out. He placed his hand on the console by the door and entered the subterranean room. 'And ordinary we are not.' The door swung shut as Nik crossed the threshold. 'You will learn our family is anything but average.'

Nik dropped his bag by the old armchairs and joined his grandfather, who waited by the steel-framed cabinet. Behind the reinforced glass was an array of weapons, modern replicas and older weapons dating back three thousand years: spears, slings, daggers, swords of various lengths and shapes, a hoplite shield, bow and arrows, crossbow, battle-axe, pistols, rifles and a machine gun.

'Do you have a licence for these?' Nik asked.

'For the guns, yes. Well, except the machine gun.'

'Quite the arsenal, Papou.' Nik tapped the glass door. 'A bit difficult to practice throwing a spear or a sling in here, let alone shoot a bow and arrow.'

'We'll use the stadium for training with the projectiles but today I want you to get familiar with the weapons.' His grandfather unlocked a door and pulled out the spears. 'Each is of a different length and weight. The Greeks used the longer spear in the phalanx formation, while the javelin, shorter and lighter, was used by the Roman foot-soldier.' Papou handed one to Nik.

'Very light,' he said, holding it in the middle. 'What's it made from?'

'Graphite. So is this one.' Papou took the javelin and passed him the other one.

'This is heavier, given the extra length.' Nik ran his hand along the smooth grain of the spear. 'It must have been difficult to control during combat.'

'It's the perfect phalanx weapon. Can you imagine how intimidating it must have been to watch armed soldiers lowering their sarissas as they charged? Not intended for throwing, rather cumbersome, but excellent for jabbing and thrusting,' Papou said.

He set the lance back in its place and then the longer spear before moving to the next weapon. Each one he handed to Nik and explained their history and how to use them. Nik grimaced as he held the pistol. The cold black metal sat heavy in his hand. His stomach lurched and a bitter taste filled his mouth.

'What is it?' his grandfather asked.

'I don't like guns.'

'The problem is not the gun, it's the person who uses it. Respect its power and what it does.'

'Why the machine gun?'

'When the guardian discovered Hitler was searching for the coin, he deemed it necessary to strengthen the firearms collection.'

'This doesn't look like it's from the 1940s.'

'No, that gun's locked in the cabinet. It's important to upgrade the weapons with newer models.'

'How big is the threat?'

Papou drew in a deep breath and exhaled through his nostrils. 'We're not the only ones who own a coin. Remember, a second one was struck and it went missing. Odds are whoever took that coin has kept it within their family. To possess one coin and use it for personal gain or ill purpose is detrimental. To own both, catastrophic.'

The ominous tone and expression on his grandfather's face made Nik doubt his decision. Almost

'Tomorrow we start with the javelin and bow and arrow. The sarissa is too long for the car; besides, we don't want to draw the attention of the neighbours,' said Papou with a smile. 'Today we start boxing, Greek style,' he added, eyes sparkling.

'I don't like the sound of that.'

Papou laughed. 'Your opponents will scream for mercy.'

Nik grimaced.

'Hold out your hands, keep your fingers and thumb stretched out.' Papou then proceeded to strap his hands.

Nik watched as Papou donned boxing mitts and instructed Nik on the basics of boxing: the stance, holding up the hands to protect the face, punching, footwork, how to inhale and exhale, and greatest impact with minimum force. He showed Nik how to jab, cross, hook, and use an uppercut. Papou put Nik through a variety of routines before telling Nik to stop two hours later.

'Go shower and I'll get breakfast,' he said, as he pulled off the mitts.

Nik nodded, his singlet clinging to him like a second skin, his face red and shining with sweat, his hair dripping. His chest rose and fell in rapid succession. He removed the strapping, plucked a towel from his bag and wiped his face and head. Nik grabbed his water bottle and drank the entire contents.

'Did anyone tell you what a taskmaster you are?' He rubbed his nose with the back of his and wiped his face again.

'Not in so many words,' Papou replied, with a slight smile.

'I think you missed your calling, Papou.' Nik gave him a lopsided grin.

'Go shower.' Papou wiped the gloves with disinfectant. 'Use the shower in the laundry.'

Nik picked up his bag and left his grandfather to finish cleaning the boxing equipment. His grandfather had installed the shower in the laundry after Yiayiá complained at the constant dirt and mud tracked into the house when his grandfather worked in the garden.

'WHAT HAPPENED ONCE the guardian arrived on Ithaka?' asked Nik. 'Did he get in touch with Odysseus's descendant?' They had returned to the secret room, the breakfast plates and coffees on the low table before them.

'He had to wait until the king was seeing petitioners, and when it was his turn, he explained who sent him,' answered Papou. 'To prove the veracity of his story, he handed over King Leonidas's ring and the note written by the Spartan. The king of Ithaka was more interested in the ring than the coin, but wanted further proof that Leonidas had written the note. The bodyguard showed him the crest of the Heraklid family, a signature used by Leonidas and replicated on the ring. Still not convinced, the king wanted to hear what happened at the pass of Thermopylae. At the end of his story, the king ordered everyone to leave the megaron except for Leonidas's bodyguard. They never disclosed what they discussed, but the king took on the bodyguard as his own. For a decade, harmony reigned at the palace, until one day the king died in suspicious circumstances and the coin disappeared.'

'What of the bodyguard? Where was he?'

'His wife was in labour with their third child and the king had dismissed him to be home for the baby's birth. When the bodyguard learned of the king's death, he commanded the royal guards to secure the palace. He searched the royal chambers, and the areas frequented by the king. He had the king's most loyal guards question the servants and members of the family. The coin was missing and so too the murderer. For weeks and months, the bodyguard searched for the coin, questioned people in town and on the farms.'

'The king had told someone else about the coin,' said Nik. 'They killed the king and stole the coin.'

'That's what the bodyguard concluded. Many petitioners visited the king daily, and it was difficult to uncover who the culprit was. It was fortunate the king had a scribe who kept a record of supplicants and where they came from. With this list in hand, the bodyguard set off to search, leaving his family.'

'He left his family? That's harsh.'

'But not unusual for those times,' said Papou. 'The men didn't have a choice; they needed to provide for their families.'

'I guess, though, it must have been difficult for the wife to raise the family on her own. Did the bodyguard find the person who stole the coin?'

'No.'

'Huh?' Nik's mouth fell open. It wasn't the answer he had expected. 'If he didn't, then how did the coin end up with our family?'

'That, my dear Niko, is the million-dollar question. No-one knows how our descendant recovered the coin.'

'Come again? What do you mean no-one knows?'

'There is no record of who stole the coin from the king, until its reappearance with Herodotos.'

'Doesn't it seem odd,' Nik said, 'that there's no information on the person who stole the coin nor what they did with it? And then for it to appear out of nowhere and in Herodotos's possession?'

'It is strange. These are questions with no answers.'

'Did you try?'

'Of course, I spent years searching but could not find anything. My father told me it was a fruitless endeavour. Many guardians tried and failed, but I wanted to prove otherwise. Your grandmother knew of my obsessive nature and told me to let it go, and in time I will find the truth. She was right, she always was.' He stared at the bookcase, captured by a past memory. 'That's when I learned of your father's habit and my failure to help him.'

Nik, struck by his grandfather's admission, didn't know how to respond. Instead, he asked, 'Herodotos must have known the person who owned the coin?'

His grandfather shook his head. 'No, the man was a stranger.'

'How did they meet?'

'That is a story in itself,' Papou sighed. He stood and walked over to the bookshelves, scanned the shelves and plucked a book. 'This is Herodotos's *Histories*, in Greek and first translation. The six books with partials from another three. Did you know Herodotos dedicated each book to the muses?'

Nik shook his head. 'I didn't.'

Papou patted the cover of the book. 'The early editions included the original headings of the books. This one does.'

Nik turned and gazed at the bookshelves jam-packed with books. 'How many books are first editions?'

'Ninety to ninety-five per cent, except those I purchased for research.'

'Holy cow, Papou! This collection is worth a fortune!'

'It is priceless,' Papou corrected.

Nik flopped back in his chair. 'This is mind-boggling! I can't believe all this is just sitting here.'

'Better get used to it. One day soon, it will all be yours.'

Chapter Eight

'Tell me what you know about Herodotos,' said Papou as he thumbed through the book.

'He came from a city called Halikarnassos, on the coast of south-western Turkey. The city later became famous for the mausoleum dedicated to Mausolos by his wife Artemisia. Herodotus spent years travelling, interviewing Egyptian priests, leaders and descendants from various families, and collating the information for his book. If memory serves me, he went to Persia, as far as India, Egypt, Italy and Greece.'

Papou nodded with approval. 'His unique style of storytelling was both lauded and disparaged. Plutarch labelled him with the moniker *Father of Lies*, and it stuck. Since then and to this day, scholars and historians consider his work as unreliable and a work of fiction.' He patted the cover of the book with affection before continuing. 'It is outrageous his latter peers did not credit him for creating a masterpiece of historical doctrine. Yes, the language and the descriptions are colourful, but Herodotus had a particular audience in mind. And like Homer before him, he wanted to captivate and entertain. Besides, he states right from the outset the purpose of the *Histories*: "Herodotos of Halikarnassos here displays his enquiry, so that human achievements may not become forgotten in time, and great and marvellous deeds – some displayed by Greeks, some by barbarians – may not be without their glory; and especially to show why the two peoples fought with each other."'

'Why do you think scholars still reject his work as a valuable source of history?' Nik asked. 'It is, after all, anecdotal evidence.'

'It is, and he was the first to investigate and collate events so his audience understood why the war happened between the Greeks and Persians. The issue scholars have is that they don't believe he journeyed to the locations he wrote about. Allegations suggest he sought people out who returned or visited these places, questioned them and recorded it as his own. Ever since, many historians assert his work as hearsay.'

'That's unjust. Who can say he never went to India, Persia or anywhere else?' Nik questioned. 'No academic can say with certainty otherwise; they weren't there.'

'Yes, that is true, however it doesn't stop people from criticising his work. But,' Papou lifted the book and tapped the cover with a finger, 'he, in fact, travelled. Herodotos had the coin.'

'You still haven't told me how he got the coin.'

'I'm just getting to that,' Papou said, as he placed the book on the table and picked up his cup of coffee. 'Herodotos was in Thurii, an Athenian settlement in southern Italy, and while there he met a man who told him of the various places he had visited. Herodotos, ever the enquiring mind, quizzed the man for he did not believe him. Several of the locations the man mentioned Herodotos knew took weeks, months, to voyage to. He wrote the man off as a drunken fool and departed. He saw this odd man again, but it would be the last time.' Papou paused and took a sip of his coffee.

'Herodotos was out walking through an olive grove on the outskirts of the city, preoccupied and muttering to himself, working on an oratory, when the man with the tall tales materialised. He stumbled towards Herodotos, nursing his left arm. An arrow protruded from his shoulder. The man collapsed at Herodotos's feet and passed out. A coin fell from his hand. Herodotos picked it up, lifted the man into his arms and carried him back to the city, where the man died. It turned out the arrowhead had been dipped in poison.'

'He just appeared? Like …' Nik clicked his fingers, '… that?'

'That's what happened, according to Herodotos.'

'Where did the man come from? Did Herodotos have time to ask how, and where he got shot?'

Papou shook his head. 'No, but the man mentioned the coin while Herodotos carried him. He kept muttering, "coin; travel". The man was not from Thurii, no-one knew him, where he came from or his name. Herodotos felt sorry for the mystery man, so he had his body cremated and the ashes interned in an urn and buried. Days later, he had a closer look at the coin and thought back to what the man said. On the obverse side, the imprint had a square divided into four parts. One section, the bottom right, contained a strange image: a tiny face from which three legs, bent at the knee, formed a circle.'

Papou pulled the coin out from his pocket and held it out for Nik to see. The motif was tiny, and if his grandfather hadn't described it, Nik would not have noticed or spotted the symbol.

'It's called a *Trinacria*. The pattern goes back to an Eastern god called Ba`al. The three legs represent rotation: movement and change. Herodotos tried to connect the words uttered by the man with the images on the coin. He spent weeks trying to decipher the enigma, but the solution evaded him. He put the coin in his coin bag and there it remained, forgotten. He resumed travelling through southern Italy and Sicily, questioning and gathering information for his composition.

'During a conversation with a benefactor, he mentioned his desire to travel to Persia to investigate Cyrus the Great and the Achaemenid Empire. While walking from his patron's home to the markets, he pulled out his coin bag and a few pennies fell out. As he bent to collect them, he vanished in an instant.' Papou clicked his fingers. 'When he reappeared, Herodotos found himself in a desert, though in the distance he saw greenery that he assumed was farmland. Confused about his surroundings, Herodotus looked for the familiar landmarks of the markets and the streets of Messene, a Greek city in Sicily. In his hand he clutched the coins, including the one that belonged to the deceased man.'

'What did he do? Did he panic?' Nik asked.

'I am sure he did, though he was a man never to admit he was frightened, and nor would he write it. He waited to see if he would return just as he'd left, but after a while realised he wasn't going anywhere. Unsure which way to go, he used logic and walked towards the vegetation hoping to find water and people.'

'Did he get back to Sicily?'

'He did,' Papou replied, tilting his head to the side, 'but not for months. Once he realised where he had landed, and after getting over the initial shock, he found a sponsor, a wealthy landowner who provided accommodation and food for Herodotos's oratorical recitations for the benefit of the landowner's family and guests. Herodotos agreed to the conditions and set to work.'

'Where did he end up?'

'Persepolis, the capital of the Achaemenid Empire.'

'No way!' said Nik, astonished. 'How did he get back to Sicily? Did he travel the same way as he did to Persepolis?'

'No, he sailed back. Herodotos wasn't sure how he arrived in Persia and thought if he went back to the same place he might replicate the event.'

'And did he?'

'Nope.'

'What did he do then?'

'He kept trying until one day he tossed the coin into the air. When he caught it, he found himself somewhere else.'

'Where did he go this time?'

'Egypt.'

Nik gave a low whistle. 'I guess he learned how to use the coin.'

'He did.'

'Did any of our ancestors use the coin?' Nik asked, leaning forward.

'Once.'

Nik jerked his head back as if slapped.

'What happened?'

'Nothing good comes to those who use the coin,' his grandfather responded in a flat tone.

Nik sat back, his skin tingling. The bleak look on his grandfather's face made the hair on his arms stand on end. 'There's more. What aren't you telling me? What trouble did the guardian get into?'

'During the fourth century CE, the Roman Catholic empire declared war against paganism. They hired mercenaries to raid temples and destroy them, the Vestal Virgins were disbanded and the eternal flame extinguished. They killed pagan priests and many of their followers. In the early twelfth century, the Roman Catholic empire imposed radical laws against the pagans. So much atrocity, and innocent people persecuted under the banner of Christianity continued through to the nineteenth century.

'The keeper of the coin, fearing for his family, transported them to Limnos, Greece. He went back and forth until all members and close friends were safe. Soon word spread about how this man possessed the power to appear and disappear at will. Wealthy people sought him out and offered vast sums of money if he'd help them leave. From the outset he agreed, because he wanted to help, but then he got greedy and asked for more money each time he relocated a person. His fame reached the ears of the Pope, who issued a decree to capture and put him to death for practising witchcraft.' Papou stared into his empty cup.

'They caught him,' said Nik in a matter-of-fact tone. He didn't have to ask what form of punishment the man received.

'The new guardian vowed that from then on, no descendant should use the coin or learn how to use it.' Papou looked at Nik.

'What is it?' Nik asked, not convinced he wanted to hear what came next.

'According to the historical records of the new guardian, a Papal soldier had in his possession a coin, and used it to capture so-called heretics.'

Nik took a few minutes to gather his thoughts. 'What happened to the soldier?' he asked. 'I hope they sentenced him for using the coin.'

Papou stood. 'I need something stronger to drink.' He marched over to the kitchenette, opened an overhead cupboard and grabbed a bottle of Cognac. He poured two fingers of the amber liquid into his cup and tossed it back as if it were water. The bottle clutched in his hand, he tipped more into his cup and brought a glass for Nik.

'No, instead they rewarded him for his services. He was given captaincy of his own squad and guaranteed land if he continued to bring heretical followers to trial. That's what's written in the history books. What the writer omitted from the text was the nature of his death, killed by one of his men en route to Carcassonne. They were acting on the orders of the Pope.'

'Oh no! Don't say the Catholic Church has the coin?'

'No, he didn't have the coin with him. He suspected the day would come where the Church would see him as a threat and took steps to hide it.'

'That's how the legend of the coin started, from those two events.'

'Without a doubt.'

'Did anyone find out where he hid it?'

Papou shook his head. 'As far as I know, no-one has found the coin. That is the reason for this.' He did a sweeping gesture of the room. 'If they discovered the second coin, we'd soon hear about it.'

'What are the odds that someone has it and is keeping it secret?'

'I have considered that option on numerous occasions. I even identified locations and the nature of a person or people who may have it. At the end of the exercise, I realised those seeking the coin would use it. That's when I upgraded the monitoring system.' Papou swirled the contents of his cup and breathed in the honeyed aromas.

'It's important you understand the consequences associated with the coin. The lure of the coin is compelling: it can promise so many things, such as wealth and power. Yet there is a negative side too. Other than greed, there are adverse effects in using the coin. The more a person travels with it, the detrimental impact on the body becomes stronger and noticeable. The details of this impact are minimal but the most significant signs are tremors and ageing.'

'Is that how Herodotos died?'

'The effects were showing, but no, he was one of the hundreds who died from a plague that ravaged Athens.'

Papou took Nik's hand, placed the coin in his palm and closed his fingers around it, hiding it from sight. The coin throbbed in Nik's fist. He stared at his grandfather.

'Can you feel that?' Papou asked.

Nik nodded, unable to speak. Though small, the vibrations spread from his hand and up his arm. His heart started beating in tempo with the pulsating coin.

'When you are ready, you will take full responsibility. You must conceal the turtle where no-one will ever find it.'

His grandfather put out his hand, palm facing upwards. Nik dropped the coin into his waiting hand. A sense of loss overcame him as soon as the precious object left his possession. Papou grabbed his wrist.

'Do not fall under its temptation. You must resist. As part of your training you will hold the coin for some lengths of time, until I am convinced of your ability to withstand its influence.'

'I didn't expect that to happen,' Nik said, rubbing his thumb over his palm where the coin had sat.

'It is disconcerting, something you don't expect from an inanimate object. My father made me hold the coin for an hour. The pain was excruciating, yet an exhilarating experience. I imagined myself to be invincible, and when I returned the turtle, my head ached for days.'

'For such a minor item, it packs a punch. Has anyone investigated to determine what compounds are in the metal?'

'In the days of alchemy, the guardian conducted experiments and studies of the coin, though the results showed nothing out of the ordinary.'

Papou got up from his chair and walked to the bookshelf. He scanned the titles of a few books, found the one he wanted and returned to his chair. He flipped through the pages, handed the book to Nik and pointed to a passage.

'Their findings showed the coin was a mix of gold and silver, seventy per cent of the latter, the dominant metal.'

Nik skimmed the text. The archaic language formal and pompous – lengthy in its explanation of the properties of the coin – and how undistinguishable it appeared compared to other Greek currency of the time.

'Didn't they experience any effects when they handled the coin?' he asked.

'There's no mention of how the coin affected the original guardians, though later protectors passed on how they reacted to the coin,' Papou said.

'Do you reckon they left out the information on purpose in case someone else read the book?' Nik asked.

'That's the conclusion I came to,' replied Papou. 'The study of alchemy drew the attention of the Church, and ordered their soldiers to hunt and condemn these scientists. To avoid persecution, further studies lapsed and later, when chemistry and science became the frontiers of learning, it was safer to keep the coin hidden.'

Nik stared at the paragraphs, trying to glean further meaning. 'Then how ... no, what makes the coin do ... whatever it does?'

'I've tried to rationalise what and why, and concluded there is no explanation or logic to what it does,' Papou replied. 'There are theories as to the workings of the coin.' He stopped talking.

Nik frowned. 'What are those?'

'Mind you, these are only speculations and difficult to confirm, not by science,' Papou conceded. 'One strong conjecture suggests the rock from which the ancient Greeks made the coins came from Kronos, the one he ingested and then regurgitated.'

'Is this the myth where Rhea tricked Kronos to consume the rock instead of Zeus, who later made his father throw up the children he ate?' Nik asked.

'The same.' Papou affirmed with a nod. 'Therefore, the stone had absorbed the energy of the Titan, making it omnipotent.'

'Okay ...' Nik scratched his head. 'You said theories in the plural, so what are the others?'

'One relates to the goddess Aphrodite, who acknowledged the homage in the coins being dedicated to her by infusing them with unusual properties. Another story was that a bolt of lightning struck the rock.'

'That one at least makes sense,' said Nik.

'I considered that too and read the effects of lightning and its impact on rocks. The heat of lightning cannot only melt rock, but cause a reaction much like a bomb exploding. To date, there's no evidence that lightning transmits anything to rocks other than blasting it to pieces,' said his grandfather. He spoke as though he were a journalist reciting unpleasant news to a television audience.

Nik looked at the book on his lap. Its weight seemed to press down as if to make him understand its message through the thousands of words printed on its pages 'You can't mean to say …' he couldn't voice the words. His grandfather's explanation sounded too farfetched.

'I haven't discounted the possibility of truth in the legends,' Papou replied. 'Sometimes such factors that confront us are unexplainable and difficult to substantiate, yet they happen.'

'You believe the Greek gods, and those from other cultures, existed?' asked Nik.

Papou shrugged. 'Who's say they didn't? No-one can discount their existence, to do so is to ignore the progress of civilisation and religions. Come with me, I want to show you something.'

Nik placed the book on the coffee table and followed his grandfather to the vault. Papou entered the code, and waited a few seconds as locks opened and emitted a hiss. He pulled the heavy door ajar and entered the compact room. On three walls were tall glass cabinets filled with scrolls, each fitted with an independent thermostat. In the middle of the room was a draftsman's table. Nik stared at the shelves layered with yellowed and brown-edged parchments.

'What are these?'

Papou turned, amused. 'After all you've seen and heard, Niko, you need to ask?'

'Holy cow, Papou! Do you have any more hidden rooms like this?'

Papou chuckled. 'No, this is the last one.' He pointed. 'In the desk drawer you'll find white gloves. Grab a pair for me and one for you.'

'Where are the scrolls from?' Nik asked as he handed the gloves to his grandfather.

'Oh, here and there,' Papou replied, closing the door of the vault. He then unlocked one of the cabinets and grabbed a scroll from the top shelf. He closed the glass door and walked to the table. With care, Papou undid the ribbon and placed the ancient parchment on the table and with a thumb and forefinger, took hold of the edge to pull it away. He unravelled the scroll with care. Nik held his breath as the black-inked brush strokes came to light.

'Ancient Greek,' Nik said in a whisper.

He sensed rather than saw his grandfather nod. 'Yes. This pre-dates the Dead Sea Scrolls. All myths had an origin and were sometimes based on actual events and people. The gods were no different. How can any person disavow the wealth of texts and evidence from ancient cultures around the world? Hesiod's own works outline the creation of the world and the gods.'

'This is Hesiod's *Theogony*?'

'No, it is a copy of the original one housed in the Alexandria Library.'

Nik reached out, his hand shaking as he touched the scroll. 'This is incredible, Papou. You own the oldest surviving text of Hesiod's poem. How on earth did it end up here?'

'Why do you ask such questions when the answer is obvious?' Papou demanded.

Nik gave a sharp snort of laughter and shook his head. 'You may be used to this but, Papou, it takes time to digest. It's so surreal: the secret bunker, the computers, thousand-year-old weapons, the rare books and now the parchments. You've had these all this time and never let on. I don't know how you live a normal life surrounded by the world's most extraordinary and valuable collection of artefacts. This is incredible.'

His grandfather glanced at the scroll he held open. 'It never occurred to me that showing you may cause anxiety.'

'I'm not anxious, Papou, more like excited and overwhelmed,' said Nik. 'I know you're not rushing me and I'm grateful you're taking time to explain and teach me, but it's still a lot to absorb. Just when I've got it under control, you zap me with another surprising and exceptional wonder.'

'You are right. When my father introduced me to this I, too, had difficulty in accepting the truth. But unlike you, I needed to learn it all after my father departed for the war. Take a break and come back tomorrow.' Papou rolled up the scroll.

'Papou, I didn't mean to …'

'Niko, it's fine.' His grandfather smiled. 'Go out and have fun. Don't worry about the coin and the guardianship: it will be here when you return.'

'But …'

'Go.' Papou waved a gloved hand at him. 'Close the doors behind you when you leave.'

'For the last five months, you've been training to get fit, learning how to use weapons and how to defend yourself if in a fight from boxing to martial arts, and you have been studying the ancient texts.' Nik and his grandfather were sitting in the bunker beneath the bathroom.

'The time has come to carry the coin. We'll begin here, under a controlled situation and where I can assess your reaction.'

'Reaction? What do you mean?'

Papou scratched the corner of his mouth before answering. 'Each guardian has a peculiar response when they first touch the coin, as you did initially holding it for a few moments.'

'Like what?' asked Nik. He remembered their conversation about the early guardians and their use of alchemy to work out the elemental properties of the coin and how it worked, but they could not solve the riddle.

Papou shrugged. 'It's different for every guardian, and there have been very few cases where the guardian did not feel the effects.' Nik watched as his grandfather reached into his pocket and withdrew the coin and held out his palm. 'And in a rare case, the guardian could not carry the coin without being crippled and another person had to take their place.'

Nik felt the skin prickle on the nape of his neck. 'What …' His voice croaked and he stopped to clear his throat. 'What did the coin do to you?'

His grandfather looked at the coin in his outstretched hand. 'I was fortunate, and the side effects were milder after the initial contact.' He looked at Nik. 'A headache and the occasional migraine.'

'Right. Well let's hope I won't be number two on the rare case statistics,' Nik joked with a half-crooked smile. He held out his hand. 'Time for the truth.'

Papou dropped the coin into Nik's palm. 'Best you close your fingers around it,' he advised.

Nik did as instructed, the weight of the small irregular-shaped coin heavier and thicker than today's currency. If an inanimate object could burn a hole through his hand, Nik expected this coin to do so. He frowned and expelled air. He hadn't realised he'd been holding his breath.

'Do you feel anything?' asked his grandfather after ten minutes had passed.

Nik looked at him and shook his head. 'Not this time. Not even the sensation of yearning I had when I held it for the first time the other day.' He opened his palm and stared at the coin and then looked at his grandfather. 'How long did it take for you to react?'

Papou sat back in his chair and gave him an enigmatic look of appraisal. 'I got a headache within the first few minutes of holding the coin.'

Nik peered at the coin.

'You may belong to the minority the coin does not affect.' Papou's voice was enthusiastic. 'But we will continue with the test to make sure. Hold the coin in your hand for another ten minutes. While you do that, I will make us a coffee.'

Nik watched Papou as he walked to the kitchenette. 'Do you know why the coin impaired a majority of the guardians and not others? I mean, are there any records or information of their reactions?'

'There isn't any documentation, just the collective knowledge communicated from one guardian to the next.' Papou spooned ground coffee into the electric percolator. 'The most common symptoms are a headache, nausea, stomach cramps and migraine, and it is common for many protectors to experience one or two of the effects at most.'

'Has anyone travelled with the coin, like how Herodotos and the guardian from the Middle Ages did?' Nik leaned forward, elbows on his knees, the coin clasped in his fist.

Papou turned, his arms crossed against his chest as he waited for the coffee to percolate. 'No. From that time on, they decided no guardian was to learn how to use the coin, and the knowledge was not passed on. Though many tried, no-one was successful.'

'Don't you find that odd? That none of the later guardians figured out how to jump from one location to another? I cannot believe, after hundreds of years, that no-one made any attempt.' Nik opened his palm and flipped the coin over to the obverse side. The percolator started boiling and the scent of brewed coffee wafted across the room.

'The predecessors considered the practice too perilous, and there was no guarantee of what would happen to someone if they used the coin. The other problem was the world's population growth, and avoiding transporting to a major city or town with lots of people. The coin would not be a secret anymore.' Papou returned to the chairs with two steaming cups of the black brew. 'My father and I believed there was a reason Herodotos did not record the manner in which he used the coin.'

Nik reached out to take a cup from his grandfather. 'And what would that be?'

Papou took a sip of his coffee. 'I believe there were detrimental effects he endured, the ramifications were too great. Besides this, Herodotos did not want future protectors to experience what he had, and also to prevent the misuse of the coin by those who wanted to use it for ill-gain, as had the guardian whose greed exposed the coin and its unique properties.'

'And in case a person like Hitler got his hands on it.'

Papou nodded. 'Can you imagine what the world would be like if Hitler or his general commander Himmler had located the sister coin?'

Nik shuddered. 'Too terrible to even consider.'

'Hence that is why I think Herodotos did not explain how he used the coin.' Papou pointed to Nik's hand. 'How are you feeling? You've been holding the coin for almost thirty minutes.'

'I feel fine,' said Nik and shrugged.

'Stand up and walk around.'

Nik gave him a questioning look. 'Why?'

'Humour me,' Papou crossed his arms against his chest

'Okay.' Nik placed the cup on the low table and stood. He turned to his grandfather, perplexed. 'What were you expecting to happen?'

'Some of your predecessors felt nothing, much like you, and yet when they moved around they experienced a few of the symptoms I mentioned earlier.' The look Papou gave him was enquiring. 'Walk around.'

Nik did as instructed, moving from one end of the room across to the other, walking around the perimeter a few times.

'Enough?' he asked as he rounded another circuit of the room.

'Go up the stairs and come back down.'

'Okay.' In a few strides, Nik was at the door. He pulled it open and trod up the stairs. The bathtub swung away to reveal the tiles in the bathroom and a yellow towel hanging from the railing on the wall. He went to the top of the stairs and then turned around, returning to the bunker where his grandfather waited near the doorway.

'How are you?'

'Same as before, Papou. Feeling good.'

Papou scratched his head as they returned to their chairs. 'You are one of the rare guardians immune to the effects of the coin, but the ultimate test is having the coin with you all day. I want you to take it home tonight, and keep it on you at all times.'

'Even when I go to bed?'

Papou nodded. 'Put it under your pillow and when you shower, make sure you bring it into the bathroom. Do not leave it unattended.'

'I'm not sure about taking it to work, it's too precious.'

'You must treat it as if it is inconsequential, an object just like a mobile phone. Soon you will consider it as a possession you have with you all the time, much like wearing a watch.'

'This is a little different to a watch or a mobile, Papou,' Nik argued. 'The coin is invaluable and not some ordinary trinket.'

'That is why it is important to adjust to your life with the coin. The sooner you accept its rarity and history and treat it as an item you wear every day, then you will no longer consider it priceless.' Papou touched his head.

'If you keep thinking about the coin, how important it is, odds are you will lose it or someone may learn of its existence, and that we don't want. The coin and you are inseparable, partners in life, that is your reality now. When you marry, then you must decide if you will tell your wife about the secret, but until then, you and the coin are as one.'

'*If* I get married,' corrected Nik. 'I haven't met a woman who I've fallen in love with.'

His grandfather smiled at him and patted him on the knee. 'It will happen. The Zosimos men always find the right woman. No female teachers at work who strike your fancy?'

Nik shook his head. 'Not really. Likeable women, but none who I want to date or be with. There's no spark.'

'Sometimes the "spark" takes time to ignite, a tiny flicker of light that becomes a roaring flame.' Papou winked.

'Is that what happened between you and Yiayiá?'

'No, for me it was instant attraction to my beautiful *agápi tis zoís mou*, love of my life, right away.' He wagged a finger at Nik. 'However, it took your Yiayiá a few days to warm to me!' His grandfather laughed. 'Now, my boy, time to show me your knife skills. Your trainer told me how pleased he was with your lessons and how adroitly you have become in the skills of defending yourself with a blade.'

'Okay.' Nik handed the coin back to his grandfather and then placed the cup on the table, stood, and pulled off his jumper. The muscles on his arms bulged, the t-shirt stretching against his well-developed chest. He strode to the weapons cabinet to retrieve a hunting knife, while his grandfather pulled out the wrestling mat.

'Afterwards, we'll practice your *krav maga*, the Israeli self-defence martial arts.' Papou nodded at Nik. 'Let's begin.'

Chapter Ten

Sunday morning two months later, Nik let himself into his grandfather's house with the keys entrusted to him when he started training and studying to be the guardian. His grandfather had given him the coin in the last month. To begin with, he kept it in his wallet, but after a week transferred it into his right front pocket. He waited for some sort of reaction, thinking by housing the coin on his person, he might feel some of the symptoms his grandfather described. Still nothing.

He glanced into the kitchen and saw it was empty, and kept walking until he reached the back door. He saw his grandfather pottering in the veggie garden and pushed open the fly-screen door.

'Good morning, Papou!' He waved. His grandfather straightened and waved back.

'I'll be in later, once I have fed the chickens,' said Papou.

'Okay.'

Nik let the door slam closed behind him and went into the bathroom. He grimaced as he walked down the stairs, and put a hand to his side. The boxing bout earlier that morning with Danny, the boxing champion his grandfather knew and had arranged regular sessions with, was sure to leave some bruises. Danny didn't hold back, though Nik grinned as he recalled a few of his own punches catching the champ off guard. Once he let himself into the bunker and secured the bathtub in its place, he set himself up with a cup of Greek coffee and settled in front of the computer monitors, scanning the constant stream of information as it searched for content relating to the coin.

Thirty minutes later, he went to the kitchenette to refill his coffee cup when a chime sounded. He frowned and looked over his shoulder, returned to the computer and clicked on the link. He grabbed a pen and notebook and wrote the details, a list of locations and terms his grandfather had set up. There was another beep and another. A series of phrases and names followed them.

Nik went cold as he went from one feed to the next. He shoved the chair back, tapped the panel near the door, hit the button by the wall and bolted up the stairs. The bathtub swung back into place.

'Papou!' Nik darted along the passageway and flung the fly-screen door open. It hit the wall and rebounded back at him, missing him by a hair's breadth. 'Papou!'

He saw his grandfather in the chicken house and sprinted to the enclosure. Papou had a fistful of corn in his hand and clucking chickens clustered around his feet waiting for the feed. The genial smile on his face froze.

'What is the matter? How many hits?'

'A dozen.'

The corn fell from Papou's hand. The hens squawked and rushed to gobble the golden kernels.

'Where are they coming from?'

'Europe.'

Papou's face was grim. 'Right, we need to analyse and decrypt the feeds.'

He hurried out of the chicken coop, rammed the latch in place, the hutch frame rattling, and the two hastened back to the house.

'Papou, you still have your boots on,' said Nik. He glanced at his grandfather's gumboots, complete with feathers and crud.

Papou pulled the boots off and tossed them aside. He yanked the door open and stepped inside, not stopping to put on any shoes. Nik followed.

Back in the secured room, Nik pointed to the first warning and the others that had followed.

Papou paled. 'Someone has found the sister coin.'

'That's what I thought too,' said Nik. 'What do we do?'

'We narrow down the location, and hope that will lead us to the person who has it.'

'Is that possible?'

'We will find the site, though it will take time. As for the individual, that may prove to be more difficult. If we know where, we can focus our search on a particular area,' confirmed Papou. 'Let's start with the first alert and work through each one.' Papou reached for the mouse and clicked on the feed.

'Has this ever happened before?' Nik asked.

The muscles in Papou's jaw tightened. 'Twice, though in both instances, there were three alerts. The last time there were this many warnings was over sixty years ago, when Hitler tried to find the coins. My father had a compact radar and by the time the warnings came through, the trail had gone cold. After the war, my father bought a British cavity magnetron that produced high-power microwaves and fitted into a newer radar model. Ever since then, upgrading technology was paramount, no matter the cost.'

Nik's eyes narrowed. 'In that case, we need to discover where and who fast. We don't want someone like another Hitler to find the other coin.'

They spent the next few hours checking each line feed, examining and cross-referencing words. *Aphrodite* kept appearing as a search term, as did *turtle* and *coin*. It was a slow and complicated process filtering out the pertinent information against false trails.

'Let's take a break,' Papou said, leaning back in his chair and stretching his arms over his head. 'Besides, I'm hungry. I work better with a belly full of food.'

Nik placed his pen on the desk and rubbed his eyes. 'An excellent idea. The words are making less sense the longer I seek a solution.' He moaned as he stood.

'My boy, you shouldn't be groaning, not with the exercise and training,' said Papou, rapping him on the shoulder.

'I'm not complaining, but Danny didn't hold back on his punches this morning.' Nik rolled his shoulders to ease the stiffness. 'I'm lucky to still have my teeth! I feel bruised all over. I understand why we're boxing without gloves but my body doesn't approve.'

Papou grinned. 'It's essential to keep fit and good preparation in case you need to defend yourself.'

'Yes, well, we'll see.'

Fifteen minutes later they returned to the bunker, replenished and determined to solve the enigma. Nik threw out his earlier efforts and flipped to a fresh sheet of paper. He went back to the first newsfeed and jotted down the location and keywords, moved onto the next one and recorded the details, until he covered each of the terms and phrases. He stared at them, forcing his mind to make sense of the words. Nothing occurred to him. Then he had an idea.

He keyed in, *map of Europe*. Google came back with over five million hits. Nik did a quick check of a few links, selected one with cities included on the map, and clicked on the print function. He grabbed a roll of sticky tape from the drawer and a ruler, and rummaged further until he found scissors. The first city he marked on the map with an X, then moved onto the next one, and continued until he had marked in all the cities. He scratched his head.

The words must mean something, he thought, as he tapped the eraser end of the pencil against the map. He looked at each keyword: *coin collectors, antiquities, old coins, museo* and *neo*, and other similar phrases popped up in the alerts in correlation to the city, but that didn't help either. Starting at Paris, he drew a line to Rome, then one from Moscow to Madrid, Manchester to Monaco, and Marseille to Cologne. A pattern formed.

'Papou,' he said in a quiet voice.

'Yes?'

'Whoever has the coin is travelling from Geneva.' Nik handed the map to his grandfather.

'Geneva?' Papou studied the lines of connections Nik had drawn.

'I haven't yet worked out how the words relate to the geographical area,' Nik added, 'or how the prefix *neo* links to each city. I know it means *young* but in what context I have no clue.'

Papou remained silent, his gaze flicked from his notes to the map. 'We need to keep monitoring their movements, this will help us to identify specific locations.'

'But why? What are they up to?'

Papou shook his head. 'I don't know.' He rubbed his brow. 'Let's call it a night, you must be here early tomorrow for training before you go to school.'

'But, Papou ...'

'Go home and rest. Whoever is using the coin will not stop and if they are smart, and I believe they are, they won't be using the sister coin for a little while.'

———

THE NEXT MORNING, Nik arrived at his grandfather's place early for training, and while his competence in combat had grown and developed, and no doubt he could defend himself more ably than seven months ago, Nik knew he had more to learn. He wanted to use the skills to protect himself as if they were second nature, like walking and talking.

Papou had Nik practice martial arts and techniques in facing an opponent wielding a knife for a few hours before he headed to work. It was the new norm for them both, training early in the morning, and then Nik returned to his grandfather's late in the afternoon to monitor the data on the computers, after marking papers.

That Monday afternoon, the computers were quiet, with none of the activity that had flummoxed them the previous day. Nik sat back and stared at the map he'd drawn. He tapped the pen against his lips and thought about how to use the information to find out who the person was and what they were up to.

He listed the cities on a fresh sheet of paper and the distances between them. How could he identify which city they started from? Nik glanced at the satellite image of the Earth and saw the multitudes of lights that dotted the northern hemisphere. It was still night-time in that part of the world. If only there was a way to track the coin, something similar to a GPS. He threw the pen on the desk, pushed the chair back and began pacing back and forth. Could the coin have some power source it emits when used?

Nik sat back down and clicked on the settings for the satellite program and browsed through the options, and turned off the tracking for planes, GPS data, military and commercial air travel, plus those for light aircraft. He then closed all external communications and downloaded the preceding day's alerts. His jaw fell open. He grabbed another piece of paper and scribbled the information as quickly as possible. The trail was fading but the destination was easy to follow. He reset the parameters on the satellite system, and with his notes in hand, dashed out of the room.

He found his grandfather in the kitchen preparing dinner.

'Papou, I worked out where the person went!' He explained what he did, the trajectory and the emissions of the coin.

'Excellent work, Niko!' Papou wiped his hands on a tea-towel and took the piece of paper from him. 'They appear to be shops.'

'I haven't checked them, but that's what I thought too.' Nik beamed. 'Whoever the person is didn't stay long either. Each spatial leap lasted maybe two hours.'

'Spatial leap?' Papou repeated, taking his attention from the paper to Nik.

He nodded, almost bouncing on his feet. 'That's what I've called this coin jump.'

'Spatial leap,' Papou said again. 'The term fits rather well.'

'Given that we know where they went, what now?'

'We fly to Europe and visit those shops,' replied Papou.

'I can't, it's the middle of the school term, there are five weeks left before I can leave,' said Nik, frustrated.

'I'll leave for Paris, check out the stores and try to learn why the person visited them.'

'Are you sure you want to go on your own? It could be risky.'

'It's just a fact-finding mission,' said Papou, 'nothing more. You join me as soon as school's finished. After we complete our search, we can visit family relatives in Greece. It's been a while since I've seen them.'

'How long will we need? I've only got two weeks before the next term starts.'

'By the time you arrive, I'll have collated the information we are searching for.' His smile made him look youthful. 'I'm looking forward to taking a break from the usual routine. I'll make the arrangements for our flights tomorrow. Let's eat first. There's a lot to organise, and I must arrange for someone to look after the house while we're away.'

Chapter Eleven

It was late in the afternoon and Nik was jogging along the Swan River, the city on his right and the river to his left, when his mobile phone rang. He slowed to a stop glanced at the name on the screen and smiled. His grandfather had left for Paris over two week's ago and rang almost every second day with an update of his reconnaissance.

'Hi, Papou! Where are you? What's that noise?' Nik asked, almost shouting.

'Hello, Niko. I am at the train station in Marseille and soon boarding for Cologne,' came the reply.

'How have the last few days been?' he inquired, careful not to ask outright.

'It has been illuminating. I've lots to tell you when you get here.'

'Looking forward to it,' said Nik, raising his voice as the background din at the other end got louder. 'I've packed my bags and they're already in the car's boot. I fly out at six in the morning.' It was the end of the school term, and they decided that Papou would use the early arrival to visit the various curios and antique stores, the trail left by the user of the sister coin. That way, when

Nik joined him, they'd know more about the purpose of the visits.

'I'll meet you at the hotel in a day's time.'

'Great, see you soon. Take care, Papou.'

'Always do. See you, Niko.'

———

THIRTY HOURS LATER, Nik arrived at Charles de Gaulle Airport, after a two-hour stopover at Dubai to catch a connecting flight to Paris. The last time he was in the French capital was five years ago, while on a holiday, and he was excited to be back. Although the circumstances of this trip were different, he hoped he would have time to revisit his favourite places.

He followed his fellow passengers off the plane and towards customs. An hour later, he was in a taxi heading into the city. The hotel his grandfather had booked was in the centre of Paris, within the Opera district. The main arteries and streets were busy, and the sidewalks bustled with pedestrians. Nik checked his watch. 9 pm. He gazed out the window and smiled. The Parisians headed out for dinner after the tourists had eaten and departed for their hotels or onto an evening event as set by their tour companies.

'Monsieur, Hilton Paris Opera,' said the driver, turning to Nik before getting out of the car.

Nik bent his head to look at the hotel. The building echoed Paris's distinctive neoclassical style of elegance and timeless beauty. The entry to the hotel was modest and small compared to the size of the facade. The driver pulled Nik's suitcase out of the boot and placed it on the footpath.

Nik gave the driver the fare plus a tip.

'*Merci beaucoup, monsieur. S'il vous plait, appelez moi si vous auriez besion d'un* taxi.' The driver handed Nik his card.

Nik took the business card and shook the man's hand. '*Merci,* monsieur. *Mon nom est*, Nik. Pardon, *je parle seulement un tout petit peu le Français*, you are very kind. I am grateful for your offer.'

The driver nodded and smiled. 'My pleasure, Monsieur Nik. My name is Sebastien. If you need a taxi, please call me.'

Nik beamed. '*Merci beaucoup*, Sebastien.'

The driver got back into the car and, with practised ease, merged into the busy evening traffic. Nik walked towards the hotel, pulling the luggage behind him. A porter approached him with a plastic smile and gave a curt bow.

'*Bonsoir*, monsieur, this way, please.' He took hold of the handle and wheeled the suitcase into the hotel, with Nik trailing behind. They passed through the oversize doors and on to the gleaming black marble flooring. The design was ornate and sumptuous, the style Napoleonic. Two chandeliers hung overhead, statues and granite columns greeted the guests with stoicism, and oversized chairs and couches filled the main sitting area. Nik resisted the urge to whistle and instead headed straight to the concierge desk, while the porter stood to one side, waiting.

The bottle-blonde behind the desk gave a smile that did not reach her eyes.

'*Bonsoir*, monsieur.'

'*Bonsoir*.' Nik pulled out the bookings information from the backpack he carried over his shoulder. '*J'ai une* reservation *au nom de* Zosimos, Iasos *et* Nikolaos.'

The woman turned to the computer screen and clicked on the mouse a few times. Minutes passed. Nik placed the sheet of paper on the marbled counter, faced it her way and pointed.

'This is the spelling of the names.'

Her gaze flicked to where he pointed. She typed in the name, her polished fingernails making a clacking sound as she struck the keys.

'*Bon*. Passport please.' She verified the details and handed the papers and passport back to Nik. 'You are on the fourth floor, room 425.' She clicked on the mouse and the printer sprang into action. Next, she opened a drawer and withdrew a card.

'Please sign here.' She marked the spot with a neat little X and passed the paper to him. 'Breakfast is from 7 am to 11 am. The restaurant is by the stairs on the right. Follow the passage, where you'll see the maître d'. Checkout is midday. This is your key card. There is a safe in your room, free wi-fi, and laundry services are available every day.' She handed him a sleek cardboard envelope that contained the key card with a picture of the hotel and its address. 'Enjoy your stay.'

'Has my grandfather, Iasos Zosimos, checked in?'

'No.' She did a quick check on the computer. 'There is a message for you.' She browsed the small niches along the wall and plucked an envelope from one. She passed it to him.

'*Merci.*'

The porter was waiting for him by the elevators, and pressed the button as Nik approached. Nik glanced at the envelope with his name scrawled on the front. He wondered if it was from his grandfather as he stepped into the lift. He tapped the edge of the envelope against his leg and stared up at the digital panel, the green glowing numbers changing with each heartbeat. When they arrived at the floor, Nik stood aside for the porter to lead the way.

'Monsieur, your room.' Nik handed him the card.

The porter opened the door and lifted the suitcase onto the bench as if it weighed nothing. Nik tipped the man and closed the door behind him. He placed the backpack and envelope on the desk and sat on the chair. He pinched the bridge of his nose, closed his eyes and yawned. The early morning start and long-distance trip were taking their toll.

He rubbed his eyes. 'A shower, then bed,' he muttered, shaking himself awake. He placed his hands on the desk and pushed himself upright, his fingertips touching the white envelope. He sat back down, picked up the envelope, ripped it open and pulled out a postcard-size paper.

Louvre, ground floor, Code of Hammurabi, 11.00 am

Nik frowned and flipped the paper to the other side. It was blank. He re-read the neat printing, the letters and spacing even and nondescript. He stared at the words, his mind racing. Who other than Papou knew he was in Paris? Did the message have something to do with the coin?

Nik placed the paper on the desk and stared at the neat script. He picked up the phone and dialled.

'Monsieur Zosimos, how can I help you?'

'May I speak with the mademoiselle who processed my room reservation?'

'Of course.'

Nik was put on hold, though he did not have to wait too long.

'Monsieur Zosimos, is there a problem with your room?'

'No, the room is fine. The envelope you gave me, did you see the person who handed it in?'

'*Non*, sorry. I wasn't on duty. I can find out who was and ask them.'

'*Merci*, I'd appreciate if you did.'

Nik hung up and picked up the note, re-read the message and flipped it to the other side. There was no clue to identify who sent it. Was he in danger? And where was Papou? The phone rang. Nik picked it up straightaway.

'Yes?'

'I am sorry, Monsieur Zosimos. The person on duty said a courier delivered the envelope.'

'Thank you for your time.'

'Is there anything else I can do for you, monsieur?'

'No, thank you.'

Nik hung up. Could it be a family member or a friend who left the message? Nik dismissed that thought. No, they would have contacted him or put their name on the note, and no one else could take time off work. He'd have to wait until tomorrow morning to meet the person at the Louvre.

Chapter Twelve

Nik woke the next morning with a heavy head. He had tossed and turned all night, worried that something terrible had happened to his grandfather and who the mystery author of the note was. A dull ache began behind his left eye and threatened to intensify. He trudged into the bathroom and splashed water on his face. He glimpsed himself in the mirror and winced. He leaned in closer, his breath fogging the mirror, and poked at the puffy dark circles under his eyes.

Fifteen minutes later, feeling better after his shower, he dressed in a white shirt with the sleeves rolled up, dark jeans and black leather brogues and took the elevator to the ground floor. The doors opened onto the lobby where the sound of voices hit him, reminding him of the noise of students at their lockers. He alighted from the elevator and headed over to reception.

'Excuse me, could you tell me if my grandfather, Iasos Zosimos, has checked in?'

'I will look for you.' The man behind the desk did a quick scan of the monitor, moved the mouse and clicked a few times. 'No, monsieur. There is no registration of your grandfather.'

'Right, thank you.' Nik pulled out his mobile to see if his

grandfather had left a message. There was one from his mother. He scrolled through his contacts list and tapped on Papou's number. The phone rang and then clicked into message bank. He decided to leave a message.

'Hi Papou, it's Niko. I'm here in Paris at the hotel, wondering where you are. Call me as soon as you can.'

He made his way to the restaurant. A maître d' was standing by a podium and smiled as he approached.

'*Bonjour* monsieur. Name and room number, please.'

'*Bonjour*. Zosimos, room 425.'

The attendant checked his list and placed a tick by his name. 'This way, please.'

'May I have a table in a quiet corner please?' asked Nik.

'I'll see what is available, monsieur.'

Inside the restaurant the chocolate-coloured seats, brown curtains, dark timber and heavy red hues mirrored Nik's sombre mood. Few tables were empty, and the hotel guests ranged from young to old, including several family groups. The clanging of cutlery and clink of china seem to compete with the drone of voices and the bustle of waiters clearing tables, dancing around the guests with practised ease, did not lessen Nik's concern for his grandfather's absence. The maître d' led him to a quieter spot in the dining room.

He pulled the chair out and waited until Nik sat. 'Enjoy your breakfast.'

'*Merci beaucoup.*'

Nik's stomach growled in anticipation as the smell of fried food wafted around him.

'*Bonjour,* monsieur, *café ou thé?*' asked the slender, dark haired waitress.

'*Un café s'il vous plat.*' The waitress poured the coffee into the cup. '*Merci.*' The girl smiled and moved on to the next table.

The faint, bitter aroma of the watery brew perked Nik up a little. With another mouthful, he headed for the breakfast bar and chose two croissants, maple syrup, and a glass of orange juice. He wondered again where his grandfather was and why he wasn't at the hotel.

After a serving of scrambled eggs and bacon, another croissant and a second cup of coffee, Nik returned to his room and brushed his teeth. He grabbed his camera, checked the room key was inside his wallet, picked up his backpack, slipped his laptop inside and hung the "Please clean room" sign on the door on his way out. At the information desk, he asked for a map and directions to the Louvre.

On exiting the hotel, he turned left and merged with other pedestrians. It was a mild and sunny day, perfect for walking the historic streets. It was the end of the European summer and tourists still swarmed Paris. The locals wore chic clothing, and the sightseers wore comfortable casual apparel with footwear suited for a day of walking.

At the traffic lights, the roads were heavy with vehicles, large and small. He crossed over onto Rue du Havre, then to Rue Auber, where he came to the Palais Garnier at the Place de L'Opéra. Nik stopped to take pictures of the palatial opera house, with the sun glinting off gilded-winged copper figures atop either side of the facade. Sitting on opposite sides of the dome was Pegasus, and in the middle, a statue of Apollo. Embossed reliefs decorated the front of the building, and Corinthian columns filled the central section, with dedications to composers and artists. Nik had the camera in his hand but took no more photos.

Another time he would have admired the majestic building, but his grandfather's continued absence and lack of contact concerned him. As he recommended walking, his thoughts turned to the mysterious author of the note. Who would send a courier to deliver an envelope with no address or signature?

He continued along Avenue de L'Opéra, ignoring the windows of the high fashion boutiques, chocolatiers, small convenience stores, souvenir shops and ice cream parlours. Nik stopped. He could see the Royal Palace and knew the Louvre wasn't much further, the traffic becoming denser the closer he got. In the last conversation with his grandfather, Papou had sounded excited, as if he'd found what he was looking for. Maybe that's why he wasn't at the hotel. He knew where the coin was and he was negotiating with the person who had it.

With that in mind, Nik continued his journey to the famous palace, recalling the one time he visited the Louvre he had lingered in the antiquities wing, his favourite section of the museum. The experience made for great lessons to teach his students the history of the incredible statues, wall friezes, pottery and ceramics, and of the ancient civilisations that created the treasures. Visiting museums was one of his passions. Today, his trip to the famous museum was for another purpose.

He joined the multitude of people at the intersection, waiting for the traffic lights to change and cross the road. The blood in Nik's veins charged as if a relentless bull was marking its territory. The crowd surged forward, propelling Nik headlong into bodies jostling for space. Reaching the other side of the road, he hung back, while the others hurried onwards.

The first time Nik had seen the former palace of the French kings, he hadn't expected it to be so large. The area it occupied was three times the size of the Melbourne Cricket Ground. Exhaust fumes from the buses, taxis and cars entering and exiting the double-arched entrance marred the experience. Nik picked up his pace and moved past the stink of the emissions blanketing the entryway. He donned his sunglasses when he emerged, the white stone walkway blinding under the sun's reflective rays.

On his right, he saw the large roundabout and the triumphal arch; the gateway to the Arc de Triomphe du Carrousel and Tuileries Garden. He kept walking, the crunch of stones underfoot leaving puffs of dust in his wake. His gut twinged. Soon he'd find out who this person was and why they wanted to meet. And whether it had something to do with Papou.

He stopped for the traffic to pass, and studied the glass pyramids, surrounded by pools, the largest housed the entrance into the museum and accompanied by three smaller ones, each positioned to create light shafts for the museum's collection. He took in the crowds of people mingling in and around the main square of the palace. There wasn't a spare bench to sit on, and many people were moving in all directions taking photos.

Once the traffic cleared, he marched towards the pyramid and upon entering, headed for the staircase that led to the main reception below ground. The area was spacious and although there were lots of people, he found it easy to navigate.

Nik purchased a ticket, picked up a map and downloaded the audio guide app. He checked to see which floor and room held the Code of Hammurabi. He glanced at his watch. Thirty minutes until he would meet the mystery person. Via a staircase, labelled 'Richelieu', he reached the ground floor, and ascended another set of stairs to the level called 'Levant'. It led to the Near Eastern Antiquities collection. He didn't want to be too far from where he had to meet this mysterious individual.

He opened a pocket on the backpack, pulled out his earbuds and plugged them into his mobile. He scrolled through the museum's app for the audio: the French-accented English directed him to the winged, human-headed bull. Nik spent the next twenty minutes moving from room to room, studying the artefacts and listening to his personal guide.

He made his way to the Code of Hammurabi and searched for the audio. The basalt stele in the shape of an index finger stood just over two metres high. Nik walked around it examining the cuneiform script the ancient scribes etched on the surface, from top to bottom, written in the Akkadian language. On the other side, with the outline of the fingernail, there was a depiction of the king receiving the laws from the sun-god Shamash. He listened to the narration explaining the contents and significance of the code, and squatted to examine the ancient script.

'An extraordinary example of judiciary power, yes?'

Nik looked up, and stood. He pulled the earbuds out and studied the brown-haired, short wiry man standing at his side. His accented English was not French.

'It was a clever and shrewd move of the king to govern the masses,' said Nik.

The man nodded. 'Yes, King Hammurabi understood the need to establish a set of laws to maintain control and ways to seek justice.'

'King Hammurabi also realised how important it was to show his benevolence and jurisdiction by placing these codes in towns under the control of Babylon. An effective legal tool and one modelled by many cultures,' Nik mentioned. He rolled the earbuds between his thumb and fingers.

The man looked at him. 'Where is your grandfather?'

Nik paused. 'What are you talking about?' The man appraised him. Nik's gut tightened.

'Come now, don't be coy. We've been tracking your grandfather for the past week. He's been asking questions he shouldn't.'

'Who are you?'

'Interpol.'

'Show me your credentials.' First his grandfather's peculiar absence, and now this man showing up for a friendly chitchat made Nik wary.

The man reached into his jacket pocket and withdrew a badge. He held it out. Nik examined the picture and name on the ID.

'This could be a fake. With today's technology, anyone can produce one of these.'

'That is true, but the badge is authentic.'

'I will need more proof than your word,' said Nik. 'I want to talk to your supervisor.'

The man frowned. 'You are overreacting.'

'Much like a stranger demanding the whereabouts of my

grandfather. What would you do if you were in my situation?' asked Nik, narrowing his eyes.

'*Bon*. Just a moment.' The man reached into his pocket, took out his mobile and placed a call. He spoke in rapid French, his gaze never leaving Nik's. He held out the phone to him. 'My commanding officer, Monsieur Dufort.'

Nik took the phone. 'Monsieur Dufort.'

'Ah Monsieur Zosimos, *bonjour*. I understand you have doubts regarding Monsieur Janssens. I can guarantee he is an Interpol officer,' the deep baritone voice said.

'How can I be sure what you're saying is genuine? For all I know you have colluded with each other and fabricated this story,' said Nik.

The voice on the line hardened. 'Monsieur Zosimos, I appreciate your scepticism, but I do not have the time to allay your reservations. Trust who we say we are and answer Monsieur Janssens' questions. Now I wish to speak to my officer.'

Nik handed the phone back to Janssens.

'*Oui?*' Janssens' eyes flicked to Nik as he spoke, and then to the floor. He hung up. 'Your grandfather, where is he?'

'I don't know, he didn't check into the hotel. Why is Interpol interested in my grandfather?'

'The places he visited, why did he go there?' asked Janssens, not answering Nik's question.

'Why does any tourist visit Europe?' responded Nik. 'Tell me what is going on, and what does this have to do with my grandfather?'

Janssens tapped his leg with a hand and squinted at Nik. 'Let's sit and have a coffee.'

They went down two flights of stairs to Napoleon Hall, where there was a café. Coffees in hand, the two men sat at a table in the busy food court. The scene resembled the League of Nations in one confined space, with a multitude of languages spoken, and the din like a passing train.

'Where is your grandfather?'

'I don't know,' repeated Nik, exasperated. 'We were to meet at the hotel but he never showed. What aren't you telling me? Has something happened to him?'

'He disappeared in Cologne.'

'What? Disappeared? How? I don't understand.' Nik paled.

'We were following him to the train station in Cologne, and he vanished.'

Nik sat immobile and silent. The noise in the café felt as if waves were crashing against his skull. 'Why were you following him?' He asked, sitting back, arms folded against his chest.

'The locations he visited are under surveillance.'

'Why?'

'They are neo-Nazi fronts. But you knew that.' Janssens leaned closer. 'Are you a sympathiser, a financial supporter for the neo-Nazi movement?'

'What?' Nik recoiled. 'No!'

Janssens took a sip of his coffee. 'Then what are you and your grandfather doing here?'

'I'm a schoolteacher here on a holiday and joining my grandfather to see sites.'

'You didn't come together. Why?'

'I was teaching.' Nik frowned. 'And my grandfather flew out earlier.'

'Why did he visit those stores?'

'Is this an interrogation?'

'No, we'd be in our office if it were.' Janssens drummed his fingers on the table. 'When will you be meeting your grandfather?'

Nik squinted at Janssens. 'I was to meet him when I arrived at the hotel. Are you going to keep asking me the same question for which I have no answer?'

Janssens ignored his question. 'How long will you be staying in Paris, or Europe?'

'I will need to contact the police in Cologne concerning the disappearance of my grandfather, and decide what to do from there.'

Janssens tossed back the last of the contents in his cup and stood. 'If you hear from your grandfather, please contact me.' He placed a card on the table. '*Au revoir*, Monsieur Zosimos.'

Nik reached across the table and picked up the card. It was white framed by a thin blue border, with the Interpol logo on the left corner and the inspector's name, Milo Janssens, centred and in black print. Underneath was his mobile number.

Nik watched as the inspector melted into the crowd. Terrible thoughts of his grandfather being kidnapped, or worse, killed, ran through his mind. Nik shoved the business card in his wallet. It was time to return to the hotel and make calls. The conversation he dreaded was the one with his parents.

Chapter Thirteen

Nik spent the next few hours on the phone to the police in Cologne. After he answered their questions about where his grandfather had journeyed, why he was in the city, and when was the last time they spoke and for how long, the police issued a bulletin to their officers with photos of his grandfather. By the end of the phone call, Nik's head was swimming, which made the conversation with his parents more difficult.

At first his father was speechless, but when the realisation hit, he got angry at the French constabulary for the false accusations. When he calmed down, he called his father an old fool for travelling on his own. After the call, Nik went out for a walk; he needed air and to clear his mind. Hands thrust into the pockets of his navy sports blazer, he wandered down a few streets and sat at a vacant table outside a café. A waitress appeared within minutes and took his order. He sat there for an hour contemplating what to do, and how his grandfather would address the predicament if the situation were reversed.

Nik returned to the hotel and thought about calling relatives in Greece to ask whether Iasos was there, but he knew Interpol would be listening. He needed to get another phone, but how was he to purchase one without being seen?

He reached into his jeans pocket and pulled out the coin. His hand tingled as the coin sat in his palm. The sensation travelled up his arm. Whether it was his emotional reaction to the coin, Nik recalled his grandfather's warning at being tempted by the unusual properties of the coin. Of its power to coerce and influence the mind. But Papou was missing and Nik needed to do something. He couldn't sit around and wait for the local constabulary to find his grandfather. Goodness knows where he was and who had him or whether he was still alive. Nik closed his eyes and tapped his forehead with a fist.

He opened his eyes and stared at the coin. I must use the coin to help Papou, but how did Herodotos make it work?

Nik studied both sides of the coin and lifted it up to the light, almost willing it to reveal its secret. If he visualised home, would it take him there? He stood up, trying to remember what Papou had said about what happened when Herodotos dropped it.

He closed his eyes, pictured the secret bunker at his grandfather's house, stretched out his hand and dropped the coin. He held his breath for a second, waiting, and then opened his eyes. He let out a heavy, disappointed sigh. He was still in the hotel room. He picked up the coin.

Scratching the back of his head, Nik moved the coin between his knuckles, thinking what to do next when the coin slipped through his fingers. He lunged to catch it, watching as it rotated towards the floor. He stuck his hand out and caught the grey metal object. A white flash blinded him and the air cracked like a whip. For a fleeting moment Nik felt as if his limbs were wrenched in opposite directions, that his arms and legs were being torn from his body. Then his arms pitched over his head as he was sucked feet first into a maelstrom. The sensation reminded him of the water-tube rides at the aquatic park, except there was no water and he was moving faster. His heart pounded against his rib cage and his breaths came in sharp gasps.

It felt as if he were hurtled through the air without a parachute. He didn't think the journey would end. With a thud his feet struck a solid surface, the jolt of the impact tipped him backwards and his head hit the floor. He lay there, willing himself to open his eyes. He couldn't remember closing them. The pain in his head pounded and his breathing was harsh and loud in the stillness. Nik clenched his fist, the knuckles taut, the coin biting deep into the palm of his hand.

He lay on the floor a while longer until his heart and breathing returned to normal. Almost. Nik opened his eyes and his mouth watered, bile rising. He sat up and blinked as he glanced around the familiar room. How did he end up here? In his house? His books sat in a pile on the coffee table, just as he had left them. He tried to recall the last thing he thought of before the coin fell from his hand, but it eluded him. He stood and wobbled, clutched his head and winced. He waited for the pain to abate and with a trembling hand, stowed the coin in his pocket.

He ran his tongue over his teeth. His mouth was as dry as the rug on the lounge floor and he went to the kitchen to get a drink of water before heading to the safe concealed in his bedroom. He punched in the code and withdrew money for public transport and the spare set of keys for his house and to his grandfather's place. Nik left the house, feeling a bit wobbly on his feet, but grateful the coin worked and hoped when he used it again, the landing and side effects won't be as dramatic.

While Nik waited at a bus stop a few streets from his place, he made a mental checklist of what to do. An hour and half later, new mobile in hand, he arrived at his grandfather's house and let himself in. He hurried into the bunker and glanced at the monitors, then stopped to take a better look. Nik peered at the screens and took a photo with his mobile. He would need more time to analyse the new information the computer program processed.

Nik went to the weapons cabinet and stared at the arsenal. He tossed his blazer onto a nearby armchair, entered the code, grabbed the SIG Sauer P938 BRG and halter, and a box of 50 124Gr. brass case jacketed hollow point bullets. The 9mm has the impact of a larger pistol, but small enough to conceal. Just as he was about to lock the cabinet, a dagger caught his attention and he took that too. He strapped the knife and sheath to his calf, covered it with his jeans and holstered the gun before slipping his blazer back on. He moved to the centre of the room and visualised the hotel room: each piece of furniture, the décor and location of the door and windows. He pulled the coin out of his pocket, flipped it into the air and caught it.

Nik shielded his eyes against the bright glare of white light, as black spots filled his vision. His hair stood on end as he was plucked into the vortex and yanked into a void. It was as if an enormous vacuum cleaner sucked him in and propelled him through a pipe like a dust particle. He had flashes of Douglas Adams' book *The Hitchhiker's Guide to the Galaxy*, and wondered if he needed to bring a towel.

Nik fell onto the bed and bounced up and down a few times on the mattress. He dropped the box of ammo and clutched his head and groaned. He tasted the rising bitterness of bile again and pressed his lips tight and swallowed, his head swimming. The nausea grew, while his body grew hot and then cold. Nik forced himself onto his feet and dashed into the bathroom and threw up. He flushed the toilet and staggered over to the basin. He picked up the folded white flannel, dampened it and ran it over his face and then looked at his reflection in the mirror. His face was pasty and tinged with yellow, making his five o'clock shadow appear much darker against the pallor of his skin. He covered his face with the flannel: the damp cloth soothing his feverish skin. Nik stepped back into the room and looked around.

He checked the desk for his laptop and, not seeing it there, whipped open the wardrobe door. He felt the blood drain from his face. He threw the flannel back into the bathroom and dashed towards the door of the room. From the corner of his eye he spied the box of ammo, spun on his heel, picked up the box and hustled back to the door, pulled it open wide enough to peer through the gap. There wasn't anyone in the hallway; he yanked the door open and bolted out of the room. Glancing at the number as the door closed behind him, it confirmed he had leapt into the wrong room. He shook his head, annoyed by his poor sense of direction and inability to pinpoint his landing. Checking again that no one was around, and keeping the box of ammo tucked up his sleeve, he approached his room.

Nik reached into his pocket and swore under his breath. No swipe card. With no possibility of returning to the suite he just left, he looked around for a place to hide the ammo and spotted the exit door at the end of the corridor. He darted towards the exit, perspiration sprinkling his forehead, and wiped his mouth with the back of his hand as the nausea threatened again. He pushed open the door and searched for a place to stash the ammunition. He looked up and down the stairwell, and only saw plain polished cement steps and black hand railings, nowhere to conceal the ammo. His heart plummeted and he returned to the corridor. Down the far end of the passageway was a stand with a pot plant on it. Nik sped towards it, careful not to disturb other patrons who may be in their rooms.

Nik moved around the stand, examining it, and swore and banged it with his palm. The sound bounced off the walls. He froze and looked over his shoulder, half expecting someone to investigate the noise. Just as he was about to walk away, he noticed a gap behind the stand big enough to hide the box. He looked around for a security camera and when satisfied there wasn't one, shoved the ammo inside.

Nik took the elevator to the main lobby, not wanting to draw attention by using the stairwell. After a few minutes of convincing the receptionist who he was, woman gave him a spare key card as Janssens appeared by his side.

'Monsieur Zosimos, I have been trying to reach you,' Janssens said. The Interpol agent's smile wasn't amiable.

Nik thanked the woman and stepped away from the reception desk.

'I've been unwell,' he said as the agent moved in step with him. He rubbed his jaw, the pistol and halter felt as if it were burning a hole through his blazer, and hoped the agent wasn't looking too closely.

'Have you seen the hotel doctor?'

'It's a headache,' Nik replied. 'I have medication in my room.' He pinched the bridge of his nose. 'Look, can we do this another time? I really need to get back to my room and lie down.'

Janssens gave a curt nod. 'I'll return tomorrow. *Bonsoir.*'

Nik headed towards the elevator, taking care not to hurry, feeling the weight of the inspector's gaze on him. He waited a few minutes for it to arrive and moved aside as people stepped out. Once inside, he saw Janssens was staring at him from across the lobby. The doors closed and Nik swallowed, feeling nauseous, and began to feel hot and cold at the same time. It seemed he was not immune to the side-effects of the coin.

When the elevator stopped at his floor, Nik wiped his brow, intent on recovering the ammunition before returning to his room. After what seemed a long trek to the hallway stand, he made it back to his room. He dumped the box on the desk next to his laptop, and went to the bathroom to wash his face. Moments later, he lay sprawled on top of the bed, a cold flannel over his forehead. Relief flooded his entire body.

He tried to empty his mind of any thoughts, and willed the nausea to subside. The impact of the second spatial leap were worse. He hoped the side effects would ease the next time he used the coin, and as his body got used to the faster than light transference.

Chapter Fourteen

A persistent and annoying ringing blared in the quiet room. Nik opened a bleary eye, turned onto his side and peered at the digital clock on the bedside table. The phone kept ringing. Nik yawned, sat up and picked up the phone.

'Hello?' His voice was a bare whisper. He cleared his throat. 'Hello?'

The phone clicked on the other end. Nik held the receiver away from his ear and frowned. He put the phone back on its cradle and stared at it, wondering if it would ring again. After a few minutes passed, he got up and had a quick shower, thinking it likely someone had called the wrong room. His stomach rumbled: he may just make the late breakfast sitting, but before heading down, he needed to lock the weapons into the safe.

'Bugger.'

The pistol, box of ammunition, extra cash, mobile phone, folder with intel and passport filled the safe. No room left for the knife and sheath. Nik locked the safe and looked around the room for a hiding place, his gaze falling to his luggage.

REFRESHED and feeling much better after a cup of coffee, Nik tucked into a plate of bacon, scrambled eggs and sausages, when Janssens appeared and sat opposite him.

'I see you're feeling much better this morning,' Janssens said, as Nik continued to eat.

'I missed dinner last night,' Nik said.

Janssens nodded. 'Have you heard from your grandfather?'

Nik shook his head and pointed his fork at him. 'Did you place a call to my room earlier this morning?'

'*Non*. What time was this?'

'Just after nine.' Nik cut a piece of the sausage and put it in his mouth. 'I thought it might be you. The person hung up after I said hello.'

Janssens sat in silence, his face unreadable. 'I'll return in a few minutes.' He left the table.

Nik blinked and stopped chewing as he watched the Interpol agent leave the dining room. The inspector's unexpected exit puzzled him. He set down his fork and knife, swallowed and picked up his fresh cup of coffee. His stomach growled. Nik dismissed the inspector's behaviour for the moment and got more food. He was part way through his second serving when Janssens returned, slapping his notebook down on the table.

'What's happened?' Nik asked.

'Have you received any phone calls from anyone other than your family in the last few days?'

'No. Why? Aren't you monitoring my calls?'

Janssens didn't reply. Nik pushed aside his plate.

'What is this regarding?' he asked. 'Why are you so interested in that phone call?'

'Monsieur, is it possible your grandfather is associating with neo-Nazis without you knowing?'

Nik snorted. 'My great-grandfather fought against the Nazis in the Second World War. There's no way his son, my grandfather, is involved with neo-Nazis. He would take up arms to fight them if he could.'

'Are you sure?'

Nik's face grew taut as he leaned towards Janssens and drilled a finger on the hard surface of the table. 'I know my grandfather. To suggest he'd mix with fascists or extremists is dishonourable. Your focus is finding him, not accusing him of being a fascist.'

'In my experience, it often surprises family members to learn of the exploits of their loved ones. Most times, the perpetrator is skilled at keeping secrets from those closest to them, and has done so for years, leading a double life.' Janssens clasped his hands on the table, fingers interlocking. 'Clues of the deception are apparent when the relatives look back at their behaviour during particular times and events. There's the odd excuse given for not attending birthdays, weddings or even minor engagements such as gatherings at meals. When these circumstances are pieced together, they paint a picture of unusual activity, which is construed as suspicious.'

The inspector flipped open his notepad and pulled a pen from his inner jacket pocket. 'Tell me, Monsieur Zosimos, how many instances can you recall where your grandfather has not shown up and didn't give valid reasons for his absences?'

Nik straightened in his seat. He recalled the time when he graduated from university and his grandparents could not attend. His grandmother rang to say that Papou's meeting with the Dean of History and Archaeology had run overtime and apologised for their absence.

'Show me a family that doesn't have skeletons in the closet,' answered Nik, picking up his coffee cup. 'It's human nature to hold secrets even with those who are intimates. It's built into our psyche, a way to protect ourselves from being hurt.'

'*Oui*, but there are secrets that can be dangerous and affect the lives of innocent people,' Janssens remarked.

Nik lowered his voice. 'Let me rephrase so you can understand: my grandfather is an honourable man and is not associating with neo-Nazis. Now if you would excuse me, I have an appointment with a police detective who is more interested in finding my grandfather than accusing him of something he hasn't done.' Nik stalked out of the dining room, hands clenched, seething at the inspector's accusations.

Back in his room, Nik brushed his teeth, giving himself time to calm down before phoning to update his parents on what was happening. He relayed the conversation he'd had with the inspector. His mother was taken aback and his father outraged.

'Papou is many things, driven by his work, but he'd never take part or be a part of such a terrible organisation. It's not who he is and what he stands for,' Leon said, his words clipped. 'I'm seeking legal advice from someone who knows international law to see what we can do to stop this insidious line of investigation.'

They spoke for a while longer before Nik hung up and readied himself for his meeting with the police detective, downstairs in the hotel's foyer. He put his laptop in his backpack in case he needed it, checked his wallet and cash status and made sure the room key card was secured inside. He shoved the wallet into his front pocket of his jeans, the coin secreted amongst the other currency, and was about to leave when there was a knock at the door.

He yanked open the door, thinking it might be Janssens, ready to lash out at him with a few choice words. Nik stared at the tall blond-haired man.

'Mr Zosimos?' The man pronounced the surname in three distinct syllables.

'Yes.' Nik responded. He tried to place the man's accent. It sounded Eastern European, perhaps from the Czech Republic, Hungary or Slovakia.

'May I come in?'

'No.' Nik blocked the doorway. 'Who are you? And why are you here?'

'It would be best if I came in to discuss such matters.'

Nik refused to move. The man stepped closer and pressed the nozzle of a gun into his stomach.

'Step back into the room.'

Nik remained still. He locked eyes with the other man's granite-coloured ones. There was a click as the safety latch on the gun was unlocked and the intruder pressed the nozzle harder into his flesh.

Nik did as instructed, the man moving with him. The door swung shut and the perpetrator lowered his gun but held it in readiness.

'My employer wishes to make an exchange. Your grandfather for the coin.'

Nik's eyes glinted. The vein by his temple pulsed and his breathing slowed. 'Where is my grandfather?'

'He's safe, for the time being. Give me the coin and in recompense your grandfather will be delivered to you.'

'Coin? What coin? Why have you kidnapped my grandfather?' His hands balled into fists and the veins in his neck stuck out as he restrained himself from lunging for the gun.

'The coin, Mr Zosimos,' the man repeated.

'What are you talking about? All I have are Euro coins,' declared Nik in an even tone. 'Where is my grandfather? Who has him?'

'If you do not give me the coin, your grandfather will die.'

Nik stood taller. 'There is a flaw in your threat. I don't have any idea what you're referring to. Return my grandfather or I will tell the police and Interpol about you and your intention to kill my grandfather.'

The phone in the room rang. Nik eyeballed the man.

'Best I get that, the concierge knows I'm in the room.' He moved to answer the phone, his eyes not wavering from his unwanted visitor.

'*Bonjour. Oui, merci.* Please tell the detective I'll be there soon. *Au revoir.*' Nik hung up.

'If I'm not in the lobby in ten minutes, odds are the police detective will come up,' he said.

The man's cold granite-coloured eyes bored into his. Nik squared himself and jutted his jaw at him.

'My employer will contact you.' The man stared hard at Nik, holstered his gun and without another word slipped out of the room.

As the door clicked shut, Nik swore and punched it. He ran a shaky hand through his hair. The confrontation had been unnerving, but the training with the weapons and education, as guided by his grandfather, helped him. He took a deep breath and held out his hand. It shook but not as much as before. Nik swung his arms. He needed to shake off the adrenaline before meeting the detective, or odds are the detective would ask unwanted questions.

A calmness and determination set in. Nik poured himself a glass of water and thought about the unexpected visit in a fresh light. His gaze settled on the suitcase where he had hidden the dagger. He would return to collect the small arsenal before taking a quick trip to Marseilles, the last place his grandfather visited before leaving for Cologne. That had been the last time they had spoken, before Nik left Perth.

Chapter Fifteen

Nik approached the concierge and enquired where the detective was waiting. She pointed to the brown plush seats behind him. He turned to see a stunning blonde woman looking his way.

'*Merci*,' he said.

The woman stood as he approached. 'Monsieur Zosimos?'

Nik nodded and put out his hand. 'Detective Sauveterre?'

'*Oui, bonjour.*'

'*Bonjour.*'

She gestured for him to sit in the chair opposite.

'Let me start by saying how sorry I am this has happened, Monsieur Zosimos,' she began, her accent soft and musical.

'*Merci beaucoup*,' he said with a nod. 'Do you have any news regarding the whereabouts of my grandfather?'

'We have the local police searching in Marseilles and the other locations your grandfather went to, but as yet they have not uncovered pertinent information,' she said. 'Can you tell me the purpose of his visit to Europe?'

'To see the sights and go to unknown places, as does any tourist,' he replied with a shrug.

She nodded. 'Did the shops he called into have any significance?'

Nik tilted his head to the side. 'No, though he likes to fossick for historical treasures. He was a professor of antiquities back home.'

'Ahh …' She paused and wrote something in her notepad. 'Where international guests encounter trouble, the police contact Interpol for further information.' Her tawny-coloured eyes held his. Nik's heart skipped a beat. 'They are, as we are, curious by his choice of cities and specific stores.'

Nik moved to the edge of his seat, his elbows resting on his knees, hands clenched tightly. The muscles on his face tightened.

'I will tell you what I told the inspector from Interpol. My grandfather is the last person who would have anything to do with the neo-Nazis, or whoever you think he's affiliated with. My grandfather is missing, and I want you to find him, so we can go back home.'

The detective regarded him in silence. Nik sat back hard, the chair rocking.

'What, no further accusations?' He stood, glaring down at her.

Detective Sauveterre rose from her seat, the fragrance of violet and patchouli arrested his senses. His skin tingled at the nearness and warmth of her body.

'Monsieur Zosimos, during our investigation we must consider all possibilities, even the ones that are distasteful. We must rule out the improbable to determine which facts are clear.'

'That should not include making false allegations about a person who doesn't have a criminal past,' he said, with less heat than his earlier outburst. He took a step back. Her proximity addled his thoughts.

'*Oui*, agreed. It is our job to check every clue we find, no matter how negligible it may appear.' She checked her notepad and snapped it shut. 'I'll be in touch, Monsieur Zosimos. You're not intending to go anywhere else?'

'Why? Am I under arrest?'

She raised a brow. Nik caught his breath. '*Non*, but it is wise you remain in the city where I can get in touch with you when I need to.'

'I will stay until my grandfather's found.'

'*Trés bon. Bonjour* monsieur, and perhaps distract yourself with a little sightseeing,' she said, as she nodded and rounded the chair. 'Oh …' She turned back. 'Please, may I have your cell number?' He looked at her perplexed. 'So I may call you direct.'

'Oh, sure.' He patted his pockets and fumbled for his phone. 'I don't call myself. Didn't the clerk or receptionist at the police station take my number when I called?'

'I left your number on my desk.' Sauveterre smiled with an apologetic shake of her head.

Nik swallowed and turned his attention to the screen on his phone, berating himself for behaving like one of his adolescent students. He keyed in his pin three times before he got it right. He scrolled through the contacts list and read out his number, including the international area code. He caught sight of her blonde hair as it fell across the fine contours of her face when she bent her head to scribble the digits. Nik slipped the phone into his pocket.

She nodded at him. '*Au revoir.*'

'*Au revoir.*' He watched her exit the hotel.

Nik slapped the side of his head with a hand, annoyed at his reaction to the detective. Quashing further thoughts of the detective, Nik returned to his room to retrieve the pistol and ammo from the safe. Since the law enforcement agencies were more interested in accusing his grandfather than finding him, Nik's trip to Marseilles had one major purpose: to gather information. The pistol holstered and concealed under his jacket, Nik grabbed his backpack and left the room.

Back in the main lobby, he asked the concierge for directions to the closest Metro station. He exited the hotel, walked for ten minutes until he arrived at the entrance to the Gare St Lazare station. He entered via the glass doors and headed for a staircase that led him to the underground station. There were people coming and going, a thriving city under the bustling metropolis. To his right were ticketing booths, both manned and automated machines. He approached a bored-looking attendant.

'*Bonjour* monsieur. *Est-ce quel* train *à* Marseille, *s'il vous pla't?*' Nik said, reading the translation from his phone.

The man's lip curled. '*Vous devez aller au Bibliothèque François Mitterrand et vous devez prendre le* TGV.'

Nik did a quick check on his phone and then asked, '*Donnez-moi un* billet, *s'il vous pla't.*'

The attendant rolled his eyes and muttered. He took the money Nik placed in the slot and thrust the ticket through the gap.

'Geez mate, you must love your job,' Nik said as he picked up the ticket. 'Pleasant too.'

With ticket in hand, Nik followed the stream of people down two flights of stairs and into a long, well-lit tunnel. He checked the colour for the train line he needed and veered to the right. As he neared the platform, his scalp prickled. He rolled his shoulders, the uncomfortable sensation not easing. Up ahead, he could see his destination. He resisted the urge to glance behind him as he walked through the archway onto the platform. A line of commuters were waiting for the train; most were busy checking their mobiles, each in a digital world of their own. He threaded his way through the crowd and came to stop a few paces away from the edge of the platform. He shifted his backpack to the other shoulder and scanned his surroundings while he waited for the train to arrive.

Metres from where he stood were a couple, dressed in casual clothes, engrossed in their map. Something about them struck Nik as odd. The arrival of the high-speed train distracted him as it whistled to a stop. The throng in front and behind him propelled him onto the train. The last few empty seats were snapped up before he made his move. He grabbed the metal pole, as did many other passengers, and planted his feet apart as the train picked up speed.

Being tall had its advantages, as he looked over the heads of those closest to him. He had an unimpeded view of the carriage. His gaze fell on the couple he had seen on the platform. They were quick to look away. He sized them up. Were they police? Or Interpol or someone associated with the thug?

The public address system crackled to life and a disembodied French voice announced the name of the next station. Nik checked the poster of tributaries of coloured lines above the door and noted there was one more stop before he reached Gare du Lyon. He stayed put as passengers disembarked and the next group got on board. A seat near him was empty and he sat on it, clasping his bag on his lap. It was not long before the voiceover broadcasted the next stop. He remained seated as the flow of commuters disembarked and boarded. Nik stood when he saw a woman carrying a child and pushing a pram. He gestured she should take his seat.

'*Merci beaucoup.*' She beamed at him. He nodded and returned the smile.

The next stretch was longer than the first two. Nik observed the couple had moved further up the carriage. When the train came to a halt, he helped the woman with the pram get off and followed her out. She thanked him again.

'No trouble at all,' he said.

'English?' she said, putting the toddler in the pram.

'No, Australian.'

'*Trés agréable*! Very nice. Welcome to Paris. Where are you going?'

'Marseilles for the day. I don't suppose you can tell me which way I need to go?' Nik gave her half a grin as he pointed at the various exits.

'*Bien sûr.*' She pointed to a group of travellers who were heading towards a lengthy flight of stairs. 'Follow them up to the main concourse, and there you will see the departure times for Marseilles.'

'*Merci beaucoup!*'

As Nik said goodbye, he noted the couple hovering a few metres away, their attention once more, focused on the map. He followed the commuters up the staircase, and when he reached the top, he stepped across to read the signboard for departures, turning his body to face the way he had come. The couple appeared, glanced in his direction and turned to go the other way. With long strides, Nik caught up with the commuters who had disembarked from his train and weaved his way into the group. Just as he stepped onto the train to Marseilles, he peered through the glass to see the couple hurrying towards the train. The sliding doors closed before they could embark.

Chapter Sixteen

The train slowed as Nik gazed out the window. Buildings and trees lined the way and then vanished as the carriage plunged into the tunnel. The fluorescent lights flickered on as the train headed further underground. Five minutes later the train came to a halt and the automated female voice announced their stop: Saint Charles. Nik slipped his backpack over his shoulder and moved with the rest of the commuters.

The platform was humming with the voices of the hundreds of people alighting or boarding the sleek TGVs. Sunlight streamed in from the A-framed windows, bathing the silver and blue trains. The heat of the sun and railway lines swamped the enormous space, giving the impression of an oversized sauna. Nik headed to the information booth, asked for a map of the city and directions to the old port. The woman behind the counter, effusive in her cheerfulness to help, highlighted the port and the most direct route. She even gave him names of places to eat.

'*Merci beaucoup!*' He smiled at her.

He marvelled at the station. It was not any different from an airport with its souvenir shops, clothing stores, bookshops and cafés, polished floors and waiting areas teeming with people. With map in hand, Nik left the station. Outside, he stopped on the paved walkway, the main road mere metres away. There were access roads for taxis, buses and a site for car rentals.

This is what we need back home! he thought, and he pulled out his mobile and took a few photos. He checked the map and decided to walk. He knew it may take him an hour or more, but he wanted to use the time to think. He needed to plan what to do once he located the store his grandfather last visited, and figure out who was following him.

The buildings resembled those in Paris, and the few contemporary high-rises looked out of place among the grand baroque and medieval structures. He would have liked time to explore the city and visit its museums, but he had come to find out what his grandfather had discovered here and what caused his disappearance in Cologne. To his left stood a cathedral erected on a hill. He checked the map: Notre-Dame de la Garde.

Nik followed the streets marked out by the helpful attendant. She had highlighted a scenic path to the port. The roads ran straight, triangular, perpendicular and circuitous. The haphazard street formation suggested that not much thought had gone into the planning and layout of the city. These were features of Europe that Nik loved: the antiquity and hidden beauty within.

La Canebière, the primary thoroughfare of Marseille, had several of the oldest and grandest buildings, of which only the facades remained. Hotels and cafés lined the way to the port; the bright and vibrant awnings jutted out onto the walkways to encourage passers-by to stop, sit and enjoy a cup of coffee. Nik's nose twitched at the briny air and he felt the fresh breeze: he was close. He crossed the main road and came to a stop. Big and small fishing boats nestled and bobbed on the water alongside yachts, most of them more extravagant than their working cousins. The rectangular port ran the length of what was once a natural bay.

He checked for traffic and crossed over to join the many pedestrians on the port side. He had memorised the address for the store: behind Quai du Port, close to the home of Jules Verne. The smell of fish grew stronger as he walked along the port. He spotted an older man accompanied by a younger one, hauling crates of fish off their boat and onto the dock. Nik cut across Quai du Port, his attention on a bar. He had a snack on the train and little to drink, and now his empty stomach rumbled. The maître d' led him to a seat by the window and gave him a menu.

He placed his backpack on the floor by his feet, sat back and stared out the tinted glass to the port. He saw two familiar figures. They slowed as they neared the bar. Nik observed them, as they paused for a few minutes. He thought they'd enter the establishment but instead, they stood at the entrance for a few minutes longer, and then moved away. A coincidence, he thought. But he did not believe in chance occurrences, especially given the disappearance of his grandfather, the interest from Interpol, the visit from the menacing Eastern European and the innuendos voiced by Detective Sauveterre.

He was certain they were the same couple he had spotted back at the Gare St Lazare station in Paris. He knew they were following him. Why? And who did they work for? Either they were officers of Interpol or the police. He discounted any attachment to his mysterious visitor and the perpetrator who kidnapped his grandfather, given their approach was more direct. He touched his front jeans pocket for his wallet, the coin mixed with other change. It may not be the safest spot for a valuable and hunted item, but he guessed that hiding it in plain sight was the securest place, as no-one would expect it to be there.

The waiter arrived to take his order and left with the menu. When Nik glanced outside again, he saw the couple standing on the other side of the road, appearing to be interested in the yachts. Two men approached them, and they chatted and looked over at the bar. Minutes later, the couple left, while the men stayed.

Nik tapped a repetitive beat on the table as he made a mental note of what the newcomers looked like and their clothing. He assumed Interpol had sent them. Right from the outset, Janssens suspected his grandfather and now possibly him, of illegal malfeasance. Or could they be police officers?

Nik glanced down at the surface of the table. He contemplated the historical information, theories, concepts and the sage voice of his grandfather. But none of what ran through his mind helped to identify who would be after the coin. He closed his eyes and took a deep breath and exhaled. Who and why now? he asked himself.

The sounds of cutlery clinking against china, the tinkle of ice dropping in glasses and people chatting faded to a dull hum. He blew through his nostrils, frustrated at not being able to figure out the answer, except for the Eastern European connection. That's where he need to focus his search. The waiter returned with his drink. Nik sat back, even more determined to find his grandfather.

Chapter Seventeen

Nik left the bar and headed further down the street. Tour buses and mini trains filled with tourists chugged past, their cameras clicking every second. Heads turned one way then the other, taking verbal cues from their personal digital translators and guides.

He arrived at the Hotel de Ville, turned right, walked a few metres and made a left. At the corner he stopped, hoisted the backpack to his other shoulder and noticed the two men standing next to the traffic lights. The pedestrian light blinked on, but they did not cross the road. Though they were a fair distance away, their presence was an ominous reminder of the precariousness of his freedom.

He slowed as he neared Jules Verne's home, and as much as he would have enjoyed the opportunity to look around, he kept walking. At the end of the block, he glanced at the signage over the doorway obscured by a leafy olive tree: the Musée Des Docks Romains. The double doors, the glass panels obscured by red and white advertising, if he hadn't checked the map, he would have walked past. Nik pulled open the door and entered. The cool blast of air-conditioning and sounds of muted voices greeted him. He paid his fee and took a map and headset.

The city council had built the museum around the remains of Roman commercial warehouses. In the centre, in situ, were over thirty large urns, or *dolia*. A few of them were intact but most were damaged, the bottom halves having stood up to the test of time. The virtual translator informed him the ceramic vessels had been used to store wine or oil. Along the walls and behind glass petitions were various objects sealed in a hermetic environment: the history of maritime trading from the period of Ancient Rome 600 BCE to 400 CE. Nik took his time as he studied amphorae of assorted shapes and sizes, hardware fittings, anchors, scales, mosaics and coins. On his way out, he purchased a book that would be a useful resource for his teaching collection. He half expected his shadows to follow him, but they hadn't.

Next door was an antique store. A bell tinkled against the door-frame as he entered. The smell of old trinkets, books and furniture was a stark contrast to the clean sterile air of the museum. Behind the counter, a grey-haired man looked up from his magazine.

'*Bonjour.*'

'*Bonjour.*' Nik nodded at him. He surveyed the range of knick-knacks and pieces of furniture – wardrobes, china cabinets, chairs, desks – the shop is crammed with goods, and the assortment of chairs interspersed wherever there was space. Wooden shelving contained a variety of items – china ware, ceramic and metal statuettes, toys, ornaments, boxes, an assortment of brooches – and coins were locked in a free-standing cabinet, arranged alongside jewellery. He was drawn to a range of ceramic wares. Few of the smaller ones resembled those he had seen in the museum. He picked up a green and black rounded sphere, the top and bottom squared, about the size of a baseball.

'*Excusez-moi* monsieur, is this a weight measure?'

'*Oui*, Romain.'

Nik raised a brow. 'A replica?'

'*Oui*, yes,' the man replied.

Nik looked for a price. 'How much?'

'Fifty Euro.'

Nik placed the ball back on the shelf and went to inspect the coins. While he had been researching Aphrodite's coin, he was surprised at the wealth of information published on the history of minting. He scanned the shelves until one caught his attention.

'Monsieur, may I have a closer look at a coin?'

The man pursed his lips and with a great sigh, heaved himself off the stool. He shuffled over, fumbling for the keys he held on a fob. He inserted a tiny skeleton key that reminded Nik of a key his mother used for her 1950s china cabinet. The older man glanced up at him.

'Which one you wish to see?'

'That one.' Nik pointed.

The man picked up the coin and handed it to him. 'This coin was from Carthago Nova, not long after Scipio Africanus fought Hannibal.'

'Is it authentic?'

'*Oui.*' The storekeeper nodded.

'How much for the coin, and do you have a certificate of authentication?'

'It is two hundred and forty-seven Euros. I have a certificate for the coin.'

Nik grimaced, shook his head and gave the coin back. 'Thank you for allowing me to see it.' He turned to leave, had second thoughts, and pulled out his mobile phone. 'I wonder if you could help me?'

The older man straightened and raised an eyebrow.

'Can you tell me if this gentleman came into your store sometime last week?' Nik showed him a picture of his grandfather. The man's jaw worked back and forth as he gave a cursory glance at the photo.

'Many customers come,' he said, turning his back on Nik.

'Of course, thank you for your time.' Nik left the store. He slid the mobile into his pocket and paused for a few moments on the footpath. The storekeeper's body language was off, he thought, and his instinct told him the man had lied. The question was why?

Nik was no closer to finding his grandfather, but he knew Iasos came to Marseilles, and probable he ventured into this store. But without firm confirmation from the shop's owner, Nik had to rethink his plan. It was time to return to Paris and conduct further research into shops of the various cities his grandfather visited.

———

NIK RETURNED to the hotel a little after six in the evening and saw Detective Sauveterre sitting in the lobby. She rose from her seat as he neared. The last thing Nik wanted was a thousand questions, but he tried not to show his irritability at her presence.

'You are working late, Detective Sauveterre. Shouldn't you be home with your family having dinner?'

'I am, how you say, "tying up loose ends",' she replied.

'Loose ends, huh?' Nik folded his arms across his chest. 'I hope the two police officers and their buddies didn't get bored following me around Marseilles.'

Detective Sauveterre's eyes widened for an instant and then narrowed. She had confirmed his suspicion.

'Why were they tailing me?' He settled into the oversized, plush armchair and stared up at her, waiting for an answer.

'I expected you would go to the last store your grandfather stopped at,' she said as she sat down opposite him.

'And you thought I may lead you to an accomplice or learn whether I'm involved in this neo-Nazi movement.' He snorted.

She shrugged. 'I needed to be certain.'

'Are you? Have I passed your test?'

'You must understand, Monsieur, we are in the middle of a war against terrorism, and my duty is to ensure the people in this city and country are safe from these radicals. I do not have the luxury to ignore potential acts of terror.' She shifted forward and straightened on the edge of her chair. 'Your grandfather attended establishments that support extremists. Why?'

Nik did not reply straightaway but kept his focus on her austere face. 'He is a man of many interests and enjoys browsing curios.'

'Bah!' She flung a hand in the air. '*Quelle bêtise!* Nonsense! You are lying.'

A rush of anger filled Nik. 'As are you. This entire investigation into the disappearance of my grandfather is a farce.'

The detective shook her head, her blonde locks moving from side to side with vigour. 'Not so, we are trying to find him. He can resolve many questions.' She drummed her fingers on the armrest of the chair. 'Why did your grandfather go to those antiquities shops?'

'The actual reason?' he asked, tilting his head to the side.

'*Oui*, I want the truth,' she replied. The detective's face displayed a neutral expression.

'He was seeking an object and information.'

'An object and information?' she repeated her eyes bored into his. 'Such as?'

Nik regarded the attractive woman who sat before him in silence, frustrated and tired, but above all fearing for the life and wellbeing of his grandfather. And here he was sitting in the hotel's foyer, being questioned by a sceptical detective, albeit a beautiful woman. He answered her question in a clipped tone. 'An old coin.'

'What makes the coin so important?'

'It's part of our family's heritage.'

'Your answer does not explain why your grandfather went to those specific stores.'

'As I mentioned, my grandfather was seeking information about a rare coin.'

The detective crossed her legs and regarded him. He sat in silence, refusing to be the first to look away or concede defeat.

'That is the first reasonable response I've heard since I've taken the case,' she said, breaking the quiet standoff. 'Mind, that is not the entire story. You are hiding something.'

'Nope, that is why he went to the antiquities shops.' Nik brushed unseen lint from his jeans. 'To learn more about the coin's history and where it came from.'

'How old is this coin your grandfather is seeking?'

'Ancient. It dates back to when the Greeks first minted coins.'

'I did not know the Greeks invented coins.'

'Now you do.' He moved to stand up. 'Now if that is all?'

Detective Sauveterre glanced at her watch. 'For now. I will be in touch, Monsieur.' She stood and held out her hand.

Nik got to his feet, shook her hand and felt a jolt. His lips parted and his hand tingled when she let go. She said an abrupt goodbye and left before he could respond. He rubbed his hand on his thigh, the touch of her hand still lingered on his. Preoccupied, he sidestepped the table and chairs and headed for the elevator.

'Monsieur Zosimos! Monsieur Zosimos!'

The calling of his name penetrated Nik's bemused mind. He turned and saw the concierge waving at him.

'*Oui*, Mademoiselle?' he said as he approached the desk.

'This envelope came for you.' She handed him a cream envelope.

'*Merci*.' The paper was thick, the grain rippled.

In his room, Nik set his backpack on the chair at the desk and sat on the bed. Apart from his name written in neat cursive handwriting on the front, there was nothing to suggest from whom or where the note came.

He ripped open the envelope and pulled out a letter. A smaller piece of paper fluttered to the floor. Nik reached down, flipped it over, and sucked in his breath. It was a picture of his grandfather, hands bound and mouth gagged with a strip of black cloth. His hair was dishevelled, but his eyes told another story. He looked angry. At the bottom of the photo, in the same handwriting as on the envelope, was today's date.

Nik closed his eyes for a moment and his heart thumped hard against his rib cage. He unfolded the letter and read the immaculate script. When he finished, he read it again and set the letter on the bed beside him. The thin, black, scripted words, their threatening message veiled by careful choice of prose, coiled around his chest and squeezed the air in his lungs. He stood, the photo slipped unseen under the bed. Nik picked up the phone and dialled reception.

'Could you please arrange for a taxi to pick me up, and call when it arrives?' He paused as the concierge acknowledged his request. '*Merci.*' His eyes flickered back to the note. The sentences taunted him, as the folded paper threatened to close.

PAN ZOSIMOS,

If you wish for no harm to befall your grandfather, come to the Musee Rodin and to Garden of Orpheus within the hour.

Do not engage with the police or Interpol, unless you prefer to have parts of your beloved grandfather severed one by one.

Konrad Resnik

NIK CLENCHED HIS HANDS. His blood stirred deep, with the veins in his arms swelling into blue, thick cords. He keyed in the code to the safe and withdrew the knife, strapped it to his leg and straightened his jeans to conceal it. He took the SIG Sauer from its holster, ejected the magazine cartridge to check the chamber was filled with bullets and made sure he loaded an extra one into the chamber. He looked to see the safety lock was on and slid the magazine back in. He loaded a spare magazine and slipped it into the inner pocket of his jacket. With the pistol holstered and spare ammo in his backpack, Nik shrugged on his blazer and checked the mirror to make sure the weapon was not visible.

He reread the contents of the note, folded it and shoved it into his pocket. He left the suite, the door shut behind him with a resounding click.

Chapter Eighteen

Nik got into the waiting taxi, gave the driver his instructions and sat back, his fingers tapping on the armrest of the door. Twenty-five minutes later the taxi pulled up outside the Musee Rodin. He paid the driver and approached the ticketing booth to purchase a pass.

The loose cream stones of the path crunched underfoot as he hastened through the manicured gardens. Around him the wide paths were well maintained, the lawns mowed with precision, the flowers, trees and shrubs tended with love and care. Visitors to the garden spread across the large parkland, their presence almost imperceptible. As he moved deeper into the verdant grounds, the dull murmur of voices was almost swallowed by the flora.

The museum opened on Wednesday nights, and at dusk the fairy lights sparkled, creating an air of enchantment. Nik strode past the twinkling lights without a second thought, as he moved beyond the marquee to enter the Garden of Orpheus, where he gave the bronze plaque of the Gates of Hell a cursory glance. Here he stopped and looked around, conscious of the weight of the pistol against his rib cage, an alien feeling yet reassuring at the same time. He heard footfalls and turned to see the blond, tall, well-built man who had threatened him in his hotel room, followed by an older, emaciated man, emerge from the rear of a conical-shaped topiary. The older man's face was angular with hollowed cheeks that made his features even more pronounced.

'Pán Zosimos, I am pleased you are here.' Smiled the older man, his voice a low rasp.

'I had little choice, Mr Resnik,' said Nik, his tone defiant and clipped. 'Where's my grandfather?'

Resnik looked him up and down. 'He is in a safe location. For now.'

'You mean he's being held captive by your goons.' Nik's lip curled. 'If you hurt him, I will tell the law enforcement what you are doing.' From the corner of his eye, he watched as the blond enforcer slipped away and disappeared behind the hedges.

Konrad Resnik clasped his hands behind his back and shrugged. 'I have acquaintances in the police force, friends in command.' He waved at the space behind him. 'Imrich told me you know nothing about the coin your grandfather owns, but I believe you lied to him.'

Nik stiffened. 'Mr Resnik, would I have come here to meet you if I knew something at all? I came to get my grandfather back.'

While travelling in the taxi, Nik had done a bit of research on his phone. Konrad Resnik was a rich and powerful Slovakian industrialist who built on his family's vast fortunes. His name appeared on many of the searches, but there were no photos of him. He was a notable philanthropist, and many websites listed his contributions to various organisations and foundations.

'Well, what a lovely surprise,' announced Resnik in an amused tone, his attention flicking behind Nik. 'Detective Sauveterre, I am so pleased you could join us.'

Nik stared at her, open-mouthed, and then clamped it shut. His eyes narrowed and turned back to Resnik. 'Let her go, she has nothing to do with this.'

'To her misfortune, she does now,' said Resnik. 'The detective must believe you are a suspect and followed you here. Am I correct?' he directed the question at her.

Sauveterre yanked her arm from the clutches of Imrich with a scowl. '*Oui*, I tailed Monsieur Zosimos here.'

Resnik clapped his hands and chuckled. 'Why is that?'

Nik glared at the detective, who replied, 'I wanted to see where he was going.'

'No, no, no, that is not why.' Resnik wagged a finger at her.

She pursed her lips. 'Fine! I wanted to find out if he was telling the truth on whether he knew where his grandfather had gone.'

Nik shook his head at her.

'And now, what are your conclusions?'

She hesitated. 'It appears Monsieur Zosimos knows nothing regarding his grandfather's disappearance.' She pointed at Resnik. 'Pán Resnik, you and your companion are under arrest for unlawful kidnapping.' She reached behind her back and unclipped the handcuffs from her belt and a walkie-talkie. She depressed a button to speak. Imrich lunged for the two-way radio.

Nik pushed Resnik, who stumbled sideways and smashed into Imrich with his shoulder. Nik grabbed the detective's hand as the two men tumbled onto the lawn.

'Run!' he shouted and hauled her along with him.

'*Arrêtez*! Stop! I must apprehend those men!'

Nik tightened his grip on her hand and kept running, dragging her with him. 'Are you kidding? Do you think Resnik will let you live? He doesn't care if you're a cop.' He glanced over his shoulder at her and then behind her. 'Move it!'

Imrich was chasing them, and Nik could see the gun in his hand.

'I am the police! I must stop him!' the detective exclaimed as he pulled her towards the entrance of the museum.

'This man will kill you and won't hesitate in coercing me to giving Resnik what he wants. The only way I can save my grandfather is to remain free. Either come with me and live, or you can try to make an arrest and die.'

'You won't be leaving!' The detective tore her hand out of his. Nik came to an abrupt halt. 'You are a witness and pivotal to the investigation.'

He backed away. 'I'm sorry but I can't.' He dashed into the thick cypress hedges, the shadows hiding him from view. He slowed when he heard her swear and a male voice shout, 'Drop your gun.'

Nik edged his way back and peered through the hedge, but it was too thick to see through.

'You have made a grave mistake at drawing a weapon on a police officer,' he heard the detective say. 'I will see you in gaol for the rest of your life, not to mention charges for kidnapping and threatening another person.'

'It is unfortunate you have stumbled into an old dispute.' Nik rushed out from the hedge and tackled Imrich, a head shoulder bump. The detective fired her gun. Imrich crumpled to the ground.

Nik kicked the firearm away from Imrich's hand and planted his foot on his uninjured arm. 'Best you handcuff him now,' he urged.

The detective hesitated a moment too long. The Slovak twisted on the ground, unbalancing Nik, and reached for his gun. Nik stomped on his hand. Imrich howled, wrenching his hand from under Nik's foot and reached for the gun with his other hand. A shot rang out.

Nik stared down at the dead Slovak. A trickle of blood dribbled from his forehead, his eyes frozen wide open. The detective grabbed her walkie-talkie.

'Detective Sauvterre, are you okay?' a voice crackled over the speaker.

'*Oui*, we need an ambulance.' The detective kicked the gun out of reach. 'Has the Australian left the gardens?'

Nik blinked at her.

'*Non*, I haven't seen him come out.'

'When he leaves, follow and apprehend him!'

'*Bon*.'

Nik spun on his heel and ran, weaving in and out of the hedges.

Chapter Nineteen

Nik landed back in the hotel room, hitting the bed and bouncing up and down on the mattress. He lay still, waiting for the wave of nausea to pass and wondering how many spatial leaps it would take for the side-effects to subside. He rolled onto his side with a groan, sat up and clasped his head in his hands, the coin still clutched in his right hand. When the pain subsided, he dropped the coin back into his wallet and slipped it into the front pocket of his jeans.

He needed to pack and find an alternative place to stay. Nik opened the chest drawers and began pulling his clothes out and throwing them on the bed and emptying the wardrobe. He shoved his clothes into his suitcase, went into the bathroom for his toiletry kit and threw it onto top of his clothes, and turned his attention to the safe. He removed his passport, airline tickets, the extra ammunition and rammed them into his backpack along with his laptop and camera. He threw the backpack over his shoulder and grabbed his suitcase. As he exited the room, Nik rang a number.

'Sebastien, it's Nikolaos Zosimos, you brought me to the

Hilton Hotel a few days ago. Can you pick me up near the Gare St Lazare station in five minutes?' He paused. '*Merci*, I'll see you there.'

He entered the lift, took the coin from his wallet and tossed it into the air.

Dear Reader

If you enjoyed reading *The Guardian's Legacy*, we'd love to hear from you. Honest reviews on Amazon, Apple, Barnes & Noble, BookBub, and Goodreads are always appreciated.

Thank you.

Luciana

Glossary of foreign words

Glossary of foreign words and phrases

GREEK	**TRANSLATIONS**
Agápi tis zoís mou	Love of my life
Gyros	Round pita bread
Keftedakia	Small meatballs
Kylix	A shallow bowl having two horizontal handles projecting from the sides, often set upon a stem terminating in a foot: used as a drinking cup
Papou	Grandfather
Stele	An upright stone slab or pillar with an inscription or design and serves a monument or market or burial stone
Stin ygeiá sas	To your health
Yiayia	Grandmother

FRENCH	
Au revoir	Goodbye
Bien sûr	Of course
Bon	Good
Bonjour	Hello
Bonsoir	Good evening
café ou thé	Coffee or tea

FRENCH	TRANSLATIONS
Donnez-moi un billet, s'il vous pla't	Please give me a ticket
Est-ce quel train à Marseille, s'il vous pla't	Which train to Marseille, please
Excusez-moi	Excuse me
J'ai une reservation au nom de Zosimos, Iasos et Nikolaos	I have a reservation for Zosimos, Iasos and Nikolaos
Merci beaucoup, monsieur. S'il vous plait, appelez moi si vous auriez besion d'un taxi	Thank you very much, sir. Please call me if you need a taxi.
Merci, monsieur. Mon nom est, Nik.	Thank you, sir. My name is Nik.
Pardon, je parle seulement un tout petit peu le Français	Sorry, I only speak a little French
Mon dieu	My God
Non	No
Oui	Yes
Quelle bêtise	What nonsense
Trés agréable	Very nice
Trés bon	Very good
Un café s'il vous plat	Coffee please
Vous devez aller au Bibliothèque François Mitterrand et vous devez prendre le TGV	You have to go to the François Mitterrand Library and you have to take the TGV

SLOVAK	
Pan	Sir/Mr

About the Author

Luciana Cavallaro, genre-bending fiction author, is the multi award-winning author of *The Labyrinthine Journey*. She has been nominated for book awards in the action/adventure and historical fiction genres, and proud of her ambitious attempt at driving her first car at the age of three. (Just between us, this was when she gave her father high blood pressure ... and the beginning of her adventures). Visit her website at www.luccav.com

Also by Luciana Cavallaro

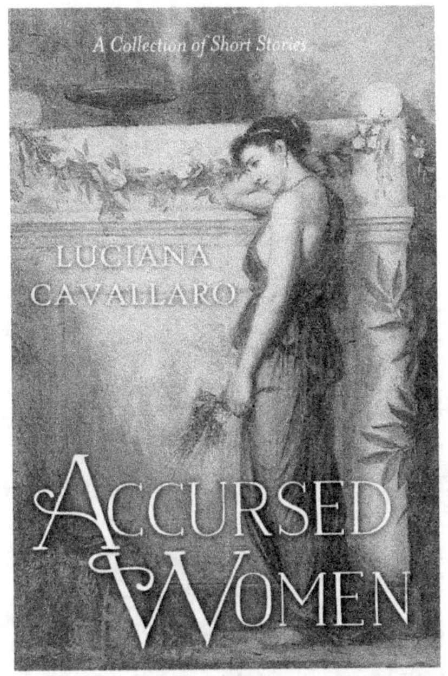

Accursed Women

Search for the Golden Serpent | Book 1 Servant of the Gods

The Labyrinthine Journey | Book 2 Servant of the Gods

For more information, visit our website.
Be sure to sign up to our e-newsletter to keep up to date
with our latest releases, news and upcoming events.